# *HEARTBEAT*

# HEARTBEAT

*Norma Fox Mazer and Harry Mazer*

BANTAM BOOKS

NEW YORK • TORONTO • LONDON • SYDNEY • AUCKLAND

HEARTBEAT
*A Bantam Book / April 1989*

*The Starfire logo is a registered trademark of Bantam Books,
a division of Bantam Doubleday Dell Publishing Group, Inc.
Registered in U.S. Patent and Trademark Office and elsewhere.*

Library of Congress Cataloging-in-Publication Data

Mazer, Norma Fox
    Heartbeat / Norma Fox Mazer and Harry Mazer.
        p.      cm.
    Summary: When a high school senior falls in love
with the girl he is supposed to be fixing up
with his best friend, the ensuing experiences
profoundly change the relationships each has
with the others.
    ISBN 0-553-05808-8
    [1. Friendship—Fiction. 2. Death—Fiction.]
I. Mazer, Harry. II. Title. III. Title: Heartbeat.
PZ7.M47398He      1989
[Fic]—dc19                                    88-31517
                                                  CIP
                                                  AC

*Published simultaneously in the United States and Canada*

PRINTED IN THE UNITED STATES OF AMERICA

FG      0  9  8  7  6  5  4  3  2  1

*For Julie and Elaine,*
*Robin and John, Norma and Irwin,*
*Dave and Marilyn,*
*Karen and Jeff: Keep on keepin' on.*

Our thanks to Dr. James Greenwald for his generous assistance.

# HEARTBEAT

# 1

Tod was a little dazed when he came out of school, the way he always was when he saw the sky again, when the weight of the day—the hours and walls and droning voices—lifted from his head. Senior year was such heavy stuff. He stretched and yawned, releasing the tension. How the future was suddenly pushed into his face! Only two weeks into the term and everybody was asking what he planned to do with his life after graduation.

He had his answer ready: "Lots of plans." Did he sound confident? What the hell did he know? "First, prelaw at State U. Then if I can pass the exams, I go on to law school."

His teachers liked that, but his father only gave that dry little laugh of his and said, "Good. I'll get a will for free."

Anything Tod said to his father, he'd get back that dismissive little laugh, as if what Tod said wasn't that much, one way or the other.

The last time Tod could remember getting along with his father was when he was thirteen. That was the year he had grown rapidly, taller, longer, hair sprouting in unexpected places. He started using his father's razor, his voice cracked and plunged. He got his man's voice.

It was a weird year. Call it raging hormones. He really screwed up that year. It began with his getting picked up by the cops for hanging out in an abandoned building. His father had to leave work to get him out of jail. A few weeks later he left his bike unlocked and someone ripped it off. His father bought him another bike, and Tod did the same jerky thing again. Then he burned his hand, and he broke a bone in his foot jumping in the bathtub, and he accidentally stabbed himself in the arm with a pair of scissors.

"They're getting to know you at the emergency room," his father said on the way home from the hospital.

"Well, I'm not going there again," Tod said, disgusted with himself. "That's it."

But that was the same summer he jumped off the falls.

It was an exceptionally hot, muggy summer. Some nights the heat in the apartment drove Tod and his father outside to sit on the steps until two or three in the morning, Tod with the newspaper, and his father with a book, his smokes, and a can of beer. They'd talk a little, sometimes about the news, sometimes about Tod's mother. "Do you remember your mother?"

Tod never did. He had been three years old when she died. His father told him that he had called for his mother for weeks, for months. "You used to wake up at night and start calling her name."

Tod had no memory of that, no memory of his mother. When he thought of her, when he "remembered," it was only what his father had told him: he always talked about Tod's mother as the great love of his life. "Remember how your mother used to sing to you?" Tod didn't. "Do you remember how she used to carry you piggyback?" He didn't remember that, either.

He knew his mother only from the photos on his father's bureau. Rosalie sitting on the edge of a cliff in England, where she came from. Rosalie, in jeans, her hands in her jacket pockets. Aside from his ears (large, like his father's), Tod could see from that picture how much he looked like his mother, the same diamond-·shaped eyes, the same greenish-blond hair, the same long, narrow jaw.

Sometimes he and his father would talk about the war—Vietnam, his father's war. His father never told him anything real about the war, just funny stories like the one about stealing a case of frozen chickens and having a barbecue on an airstrip. But Tod knew that his father's best friend, Richie Gribble, had been killed in that war. He might even have died in his father's arms. Tod wasn't sure about that part. He might have made it up himself.

Richie's picture was right next to his mother's picture on the bureau: Richie and his father with their arms around each other, both of them barefoot. Tod used to think a lot about war—would he be brave enough? He didn't like fights, he avoided them. He was big for his age and kids got the wrong idea about him. They thought he would fight, but he never did.

"War is stupid. The big countries beat up the little ones, Dad. The little ones beat on each other. The trick is to get everyone to fight by rules, like in sports. Instead of killing, they could play a game and the winner would win the war."

There was a little smile under his father's mustache.

"You can laugh, Dad, I know it's never happened, but—"

"I'm not laughing," his father protested. "I think it's a great idea." Then laughing openly, he said, "And when they run the wars like the Olympic games, I'll appoint you the umpire."

Tod leaned back and shut his eyes. The Umpire of Wars. The whistle-blower. The judge laying down the law. *You're out! Penalty! I award two free throws to the nation of . . . of . . .* Later his father half carried, half pushed Tod up to bed.

What Tod remembered best from those nights was the smell of his father—soap, cigarettes, and the sharp smell of oily machines. That summer his father was working in a welding shop, and they were living on Elizabeth Street. Six months earlier his father had been working construction and they'd lived on Pearl Street. The year before on Racine Boulevard; the year before that—he'd forgotten already.

Tod didn't like to move, but it made his father happy. He liked packing up their stuff in cardboard boxes and loading the back of the car and the U-Haul. The two of them had done it a hundred times, his father whistling as he ran up and down the stairs, talking nonstop, telling Tod how great the new apartment was going to be, how many windows there were, and how much room Tod would have for his aquariums and cages.

Every time they moved, they left something behind—a chair, a bureau, dishes. His father said it was too much junk to drag along. And they left other stuff, too, stuff you couldn't see, like Tod's waking up in his room on Higgins Street and seeing the sun creep across the wall, or the smell from the coffee factory when they lived over on the other side of Emmett Boulevard, or hearing the old lady at the newsstand say, "And how are you, Mr. Ellerbee?" every morning when Tod passed on his way to Jefferson Middle School.

But the worst part of moving was being in a new neighborhood. Nobody liked a stranger. On Elizabeth Street, Tod felt the eyes on his back, and he straightened up and swaggered and put a little sway into his walk, like *don't mess with me.*

The first kid he met on the block was Amos Vaccaro. His parents had a grocery store on the corner of Jenks and Park. There was always a Vaccaro in the store—Amos, or his twin sister, Amy, or his brother, or one of their parents. They lived over the store, and house and store, up and down, smelled of cheese and salami and the catbox in the storeroom.

It was Amos who told Tod about the falls. "That's the only place to swim, man! You been there yet?" Amos was an undersized enthusiastic bunch of bones. He was a couple of years younger than Tod. "You gotta go there. You got a bike?" Tod shook his head. "You need a bike to get there. I'll ride you over anytime I'm not working in the store. You just call me. Just call me, okay?" He was like that all the time, enthusiastic and wired up.

To get to the falls Amos and Tod rode and then walked through a big, weedy field, past the overgrown foundations of an old brick factory. By the time they reached the falls, they were sweating and itchy from insects. There were signs posted all over. KEEP OUT! NO SWIMMING! NO JUMPING! Tod could hardly wait to tear off his clothes and get into the water.

"See those kids?" Amos pointed to the top of the falls. "See that guy up there? He's going to jump."

Tod shaded his eyes, and looked up at the white rushing water. As he watched, a boy on top of the falls gave a Tarzan yell and jumped. His arms and legs churned in the air. He crashed into the water.

Tod was a little shaken up. Could *he* do something that daring? The pool was shallow at the edges and full of rocks. "Did you ever jump?" he asked Amos.

"Hey, man, I can't even swim." Amos slung an arm across Tod's shoulder. "I do a terrific dog paddle, though."

Every hot day that summer, Tod went to the falls. He climbed to the top a few times and looked down into the water. The unwritten rule was that nobody could jump until they were fifteen. Would he do it then? Could he do it? Was he brave enough? He thought of Richie Gribble, his father's friend.

Lying in bed at night or watching TV, waiting for his father to come home, the same questions came to him. Was he brave? Was he brave enough? And then other questions about the future would get mixed in there, one after another. How would he live? Would he be happy? Would he always be lonely? Was this his real life? And he'd think of his mother. If she had lived, everything would be different.

Once he saw a boy named Manny Garcia on top of the falls standing at the edge and then stepping off. The jump was so quiet. Not a sound. For a moment Manny seemed to hang in the air, arms spread like a bird making up its mind which way to fly.

It was beautiful, and the thought came to Tod that, right then, in that tiny fraction of a second, Manny could have flown out, sailed over them all, flown off into another life, maybe his real life.

His *real life*. Everything in Tod's life was so temporary. He and his father had made so many moves. Amos had lived in the same house all his life, but Tod couldn't even imagine such a thing. His *real life*. What was his real, authentic, genuine life? Was it going to come along one day and shake hands with him? Or maybe hit him in the face? Or wrap itself around him like a wet newspaper?

One day he scrambled over the rocks, climbed to the top of the falls, and eased his way to the jumping place. The older kids were up there. Tod stood at the edge, his toes in the smooth hollowed-out rock. In the distance he saw the thin silver rim of a lake and the long chimney of a factory. "Hey, kid! Get away from there." It was one of the older boys.

Tod jumped. The sun glinted on the water; he saw the circle of trees around him and the rocks below. It wasn't beautiful, and he wasn't a bird and he didn't fly. He went down, and it was bad. He hit the water off center, sideways, hit his head on a rock.

When he came to, he was flat on the ground and someone was sitting on his back, pounding on him. He gagged, threw up. Water spilled out of his mouth.

"Tod!" Amos shook him. "Tod, you want to go to the hospital?"

Tod sat up. He held his head. "No, I'm all right." He got to his feet, then sat down again. There was blood on his hand. He was dizzy and felt sick to his stomach.

Amos took off his shirt and tied it around Tod's head.

"He saved you," somebody said.

Kids crowded around.

"Amos saved you." They were all talking at once, telling Tod it had been Amos who saved him. Amos, who couldn't swim, had jumped into the pool and found Tod on the bottom. "I grabbed you and I brought you up," Amos said. "I don't know how I did it."

"I don't know what to tell you, Amos," Tod said after. "I don't know what to say." And then he did. "If you ever need me, if you ever want me, I'm your man."

Years passed before Amos asked Tod for anything.

# 2

A line of yellow school buses waited at the curb. Kids pushed around Tod as he walked toward the parking lot. A girl knocked into him, then joined several other girls standing by the brick wall. They whispered and glanced toward Tod. His neck itched; there was a bristling at the back of his head. He straightened up, slapped his pockets, as if searching for his house key. Great! Four junior-high-school girls had set off his alarms. One of them was beautiful, one was tall, one was in pigtails. Pigtails looked right at him and said, "Help! He's so gorgeous!"

It scared him—a damaging thing to admit. Seventeen years old, a senior, and still afraid of girls. He was interested, all right, and he got more interested every year. There was always one girl who commanded his attention, who stood out from the crowd and was the center of his fevered fantasies.

He'd notice everything about her—how she held her hair back with ribbons or just wore it loose, or if she painted her fingernails, or even the color of her socks. Sometimes he and *the* girl would be caught together when

9

the bell rang, and she—whoever the she was—would be so close he could touch her. Sometimes there'd be a look that he thought about for a long time.

It was Leoni Cramer last year in his tenth-grade history class. For a whole week she said hello to him every morning. Then she asked him to go to the movies. She had big green eyes, and he was ready to fall in love with her. But the date was a disaster. He blamed himself. Everything he thought to say seemed stupid, so he said nothing. He said nothing all evening. The silence grew, and he was afraid to look at Leoni.

When he left her at her house, she flung her hair back and said, "You know what? You good-looking guys are all alike. There you go through life, tall and remote. Gorgeous, aren't you? You know it. But you're really a creep. You and that aloof sneering face of yours. You're the most distant, cold boy I've ever met. Your personality is nothing, Tod Ellerbee. Zero to the tenth degree. I must have been crazy to ask you out."

He went home and looked in the bathroom mirror. His father wasn't home, but he shut the door anyway and studied his face. Yes, it was there, a superior, supercilious expression that he'd never been aware of before. He didn't feel that way inside, but there it was, on his face, as much a part of him as his big ears. A sneer—definitely a sneer. In a way he liked it. It was an impressive sneer. It gave him character. It said, Leoni Cramer, to hell with you!

One time he'd tried to tell Amos about his feelings and how uneasy he was around girls.

Amos had scoffed disbelievingly. "Come on, man! Don't put me on!"

"No, I mean it. You think you're the only one who's scared?"

"Me?" Amos clutched his heart. His legs sagged and the corners of his mouth turned down. Amos was an actor. He was always acting, always performing. Last year he'd been voted Class Ham at Bishop Hayes.

"I'm not *scared* of girls, man. It's a million times worse than that. I'm every girl's best little buddy. Girls don't think of me the way they do you." Then he turned those shining dark eyes on Tod and went into one of his embarrassing you're-my-hero, you-can-do-no-wrong, all-the-women-adore-you performances.

The junior high girls were definitely looking at Tod. Pigtails, the one who had said *Help!*, was smiling nonstop. He waved to her, and she "fainted" into her friends' arms.

It was quiet in the apartment when Tod got home. Downstairs, he heard their landlord's German shepherd moving around. Then the rabbit started thumping in the cage on the back porch. Tod shredded a head of lettuce and went out to feed him. He had found the rabbit a few weeks before, lamed, hiding under some bushes. While he cleaned the cage, he let the rabbit hop around the porch. A few days more and he'd release it.

He always had some animal or other around, white mice and hamsters. One year in grade school he had kept a cricket in his pocket. He'd had a frog and salamanders in an aquarium until he got tired of catching flies for them.

Later Amos called. "Tod, it's me. I want to talk to you, man."

Tod opened the refrigerator. He had a choice of stale bread or an open can of spaghetti sauce. He dumped sauce on the bread. "Okay, talk."

"Not on the phone. It's too personal. When're you coming over?"

Tod held the phone between his chin and shoulder and bit into the sandwich. "I'm meeting my father. We're eating out."

"Where, this time?"

"Bruno's," Tod said. "Did your mother make bread today? Save me some. I'll come over later."

He waited for his father across the street from the plant. Fairbanks Automated Gear made parts for the military. His father was a quality control inspector. Would he be in a good mood? Tod hoped they didn't end up in an argument, or worse, a nonargument, with his father dismissing everything Tod said.

His father came out of the plant with his arm around a woman.

"Who was that?" Tod asked when he got in the car.

"You mean Martha? A friend. Another inspector."

"How good a friend?"

His father took a cigarette from the pack on the dashboard. "Good friend," he said.

"Good as Loretta?"

"Depends what you mean by 'good.' " He pushed in the cigarette lighter.

Tod let the subject drop. He didn't really want to know about his father and his women. If his mother had lived . . . a lot of Tod's thoughts began with that. His parents had met when they were both working for General Electric in Schenectady, New York. His father was working as an engineer. His mother worked in the print room. Two weeks after they met, they got married. Tod was born a year later. His mother died when he was three. And his father, in his words, "hit bottom." He sold their house, gave up his job, took Tod and moved to another city, where he started a whole different life. He never worked as an engineer again, never again owned a house, a new car, a new anything.

It was eight o'clock before Tod got over to the Vaccaros'. The grocery was open and filled with the smell of freshly baked bread. As Tod started up the stairs, Amos's older brother Nick was coming down. He had a long carpenter's toolbox on his shoulder. "How's it going, Tod?"

"How about you?" Tod held the door for him. Upstairs, he knocked, then walked in. "Amos?" The apartment was noisy and overheated, with clocks ticking everywhere and three TVs playing. Amy came out of her bedroom and slapped hands with him. She was Amos's twin, but they didn't look much alike, even though they both had the dark Vaccaro eyes and springy hair.

"I haven't seen you for a while, Toddle," she said. She was wearing a T-shirt with a picture of Einstein across the front.

"I've been busy with a rabbit."

"Another rescue operation?"

Amos came out of the kitchen. "There you are, man!" He handed Tod a piece of hot buttered bread.

They went down the stairs, Amos first. Tod restrained an impulse to pat him on the head. In the last couple of years he and Amos had both grown, Tod more than Amos. He was over six feet, but Amos was still short for his age and sensitive about it.

The last time Tod had patted him on the head, they'd almost gotten into a fight. "Hands off, man," Amos had said. Tod had thought he was joking and did it again. Amos was always kidding around. But that time he exploded. "I said, cut it out! I'm not your puppy, goddamnit."

Tod had backed off, hands raised. "Hey, hey. Sorry."

They went out through the store. Mrs. Vaccaro was at the cash register. "Tod," she called, "come here. I want to ask you something. What's tofu?"

"I think it's something to eat, Mrs. Vaccaro."

"I knew that much already." She was wearing black pants and a black sweater with the sleeves pushed up. She was like a plumper, older version of Amy. "I like to help my customers out, but where am I supposed to get tofu? I tell them we're not running a supermarket, we're just a small neighborhood store." She straightened Amos's collar. "Where are you two boys going? Amos, you be home by eleven."

"Yeah, Ma," Amos said. She swatted him on the butt, and they both laughed, identical high barking laughs.

Outside, Tod and Amos walked up toward Highland Avenue. "I want to show you something, Tod," Amos said. Halfway up the hill, near the cemetery, he pointed to a yellow house with scaffolding on the driveway side. "Nick's doing the work for them," he said. The yellow house stood out like a jewel between the old dim houses on either side.

"Nice place," Tod said. "Why'd you want me to see this?"

"This girl I like lives here. She's older than me. Do you think that matters?"

"A lot of women like younger men."

Amos looked happy for a moment, then he said, "Girls think I'm cute, man, like a baby brother. *Cute.*" He grimaced. "I found out she goes to the same school you do, Tod." He pulled Tod behind a tree. "I think she's looking out the window. Don't look, man! I don't want her to know I'm hanging around outside her house . . . Her name is Hilary Goodman. Do you know her?"

"Kennedy is a big school, Amos."

"She's a junior. She works at Carl's Automotive down on Valley Drive."

"What'd you say her first name was? Helene?"

"No! Hilary! Hilary! Hilary!" He staggered around, slapping himself on the chest. "My sweet Hilary!" When Tod started to laugh, Amos said, "That's my problem, man. That's my whole problem, I can't be serious."

"Sure you can," Tod said.

"No, man, I know myself." He gripped Tod's arm. "I want you to talk to Hilary for me. Tell her about me, man. Tell her how I feel about her."

"I can't do that, Amos. Why should she listen to anything I say?"

"I've thought the whole thing over, man. If I try to talk to her, I'll wreck it. I'll make stupid jokes, and she'll laugh, but she won't think about me *that way*. You know what I mean, the way girls think about you. All you have to do is tell her I'm not just a jerk who's always making jokes. You'll know what to say."

"Amos," Tod began, "I can't—"

"I never asked you for anything before," Amos said.

And then Tod remembered. *If you ever need . . . if you ever want . . . I'm your man . . .*

# 3

When the wind blows, I smell the hospital. Mom says the hospital is too far away to smell it, but she's wrong—I have that smell right in my nose, that hospital smell that's clean and disgusting at the same time. Tonight is a year since Nana died. I can't sleep. I keep remembering Nana lying in the hospital bed, her long beautiful hair damp and clumped together and sticking to the sheets.

If only she were here with us now. She would love this house, the porches and the banister that curves up through the center of the house. The front room would be perfect for her. Her geraniums in the windows . . . when she didn't feel well, she could watch what was happening out on the street. It must have been horribly boring for her in our just-like-everyone-else's ranch house in Brookside. Nobody for her to talk to—and she liked people so much.

After we came here, I asked Mom why we ever moved to the suburbs. "Because it was a great place to bring up you and your sister. Safe and green. How can you beat that, Hilary?"

You can beat it by moving back into the city. I only wish Mom and Dad had done it years ago. Here in the city everyone doesn't look and act like everyone else. I like everything about

the city better. Kennedy High much *better than my old subur-*
*ban school. The little stores and bakeries* much *better than the*
*malls. Here, just taking a walk is interesting. And could I ever*
*have gotten my job in Brookside? Never.*

*If only Nana were here! I miss her so much. I miss talking*
*things over with her . . . and I miss brushing her hair. When I*
*was little, she used to tease me, tell me to pull her hair. "Go*
*ahead. You see how tough it is? It would make strong rope.*
*Should I cut it off and give it to the rope people?"*

*"Nana! No!" I'd cry, and I'd make her promise never to*
*give her hair away for rope.*

*"Oh . . . well, okay," she'd say. "You win." And I*
*remember how powerful that made me feel.*

*I'll never get used to her being gone.*

# 4

Friday when Tod came out of school he noticed the four junior high girls. He wound the chain around his bike seat. "Tod . . . Oh, Tod Ellerbeeeee . . . ," they called together. He waved to them. They shrieked like a flock of birds as he rode off.

The boss was at the bowling alley when Tod got there. Barry Esposito owned the place, but Loretta, his father's girlfriend, was Tod's real boss. Before Tod came to work for her, Loretta had been running the place single-handed, handing out the score sheets, renting shoes, making the sandwiches, even bringing around the soft drinks and beer. She finally told Barry either he let her hire somebody part-time or she was quitting.

Barry had another, bigger operation in the suburbs, but the way he talked, you'd think he was going on welfare tomorrow. "The bowling business is dying." He poured two sugars into the coffee Tod had served him. "I don't know why I keep this place open."

"Could it be because you're making money?" Loretta said.

18

Tod gave Loretta the thumbs-up sign. She was cute, short and chunky with droopy blue eyes.

Barry checked the cash register. "You call that money, Loretta?"

"Yeah, I call that money," Loretta said. "What do you call it?"

"I call it pitiful." He banged the register shut. "Nobody bowls anymore," he said, "it's all health clubs and exercise classes and aerobics now. And you have to have a track and a swimming pool to satisfy them." His heavy, square face was peppered with black marks. "In the old days, we set pins by hand, Tod."

"Wild," Tod said, going behind the counter to wash glasses.

"Pinboys, Tod. You ever hear of them? If you weren't fast, you got the ball right down your throat. You worked two alleys. Set one, swing over and set the other. And keep your eye on the guy with the ball."

"That man makes me nervous," Loretta said, after Barry left. "He told me when he hired me that this was a break-even operation. What's he crying about? He even makes money sometimes. I ought to open my own business, get out of this racket. One of these days I'm going to come in here and find the joint shut up tight." She snapped her fingers. "Just like that, no job."

Tod rinsed a glass. "Sweetheart," he said between his front teeth, like Humphrey Bogart, "why don't you and me take a powder, just the two of us?"

She laughed. "I'll keep it in mind, hon."

His ears heated up. He had a crush on Loretta. It was really stupid of him. Her son, Scott, was almost his age.

"Where's your dad?" she said later. For a couple of hours they'd been too busy to talk. "He said he was going to pick up Chinese takeout and come over."

Tod emptied the trash into a black plastic sack and twisted a tie around the top. "Maybe he was held up."

"By a female robber?"

Tod remembered the woman he'd seen his father with the other day. "Well, why do you put up with it?" he said. "You two are supposed to be going together."

She shrugged. "You'll understand when you're older."

Ouch. He grabbed a broom and began sweeping.

The phone rang early the next morning. "Did you see her? Did you talk to her?" Amos said. "Isn't she beautiful?"

Tod yawned. "I haven't seen your friend yet, Amos."

"What are you waiting for, man?"

"I'm going to do it." Tod reached across the counter and turned off the coffeepot. "Something like this you've got to do tactfully, Amos. You can't just blunder in."

"I know, man," Amos said. "You're right. I'm leaving it up to you. I'm depending on you."

"Who was on the phone?" Tod's father asked.

"Amos. . . . Where'd you eat last night?"

"Ling-Ling's." His father poured coffee. "You making toast?"

Tod popped the bread into the toaster. "Loretta thought you were coming over to the alleys."

"I didn't say I would. I met a friend . . ."

"Another friend?"

His father sipped his coffee. "I have more than one friend," he said after a moment.

"Lucky you."

"Right. Lucky me. Loretta is my friend. Martha is a friend. So's Patricia."

Patricia. First time Tod had heard that name.

"Half the people in the world are women," his father said.

"I've noticed."

"And unlike you, I'm not able to ignore fifty percent of the population."

Tod's neck, his ears, his whole head, got hot. *Damn it*, he thought, *what do you know about it!*

The girl with the braids stopped him in the hall. "Tod?" she said. "I'm Jen Kopp. My girlfriends said I wouldn't have the nerve to talk to you. The four of us decided—can you guess what we decided? Are you ready for this?" As she talked, she tugged at one of her braids. "We're the official Tod Ellerbee Fan Club."

"You're what?" he said

"The official Tod Ellerbee Fan Club. Your ice cream is dripping." He was eating an ice cream bar. She whipped out a tissue and wiped his sweater. "We picked you out because—taaa daaa!—we all . . . because—" Her poise deserted her for a moment. Color rushed to her cheeks. "Because you're so good-looking. The official Tod Ellerbee Fan Club knows all about you. We know where you live. We know your birthday. We even know you jumped off the falls."

"How do you know that?"

"Marilee's cousin goes to Bishop Hayes, and she knows somebody who knows you who told her. And we know you're shy and you don't have a girlfriend," she rushed on. "And you don't smile a lot, and we think you're terribly nice and sexy, and we like your casual style of dress and the way you walk, and we're your fans. Did I say that? Oh, this is so embarrassing!" Then she was off again. "We have a contest to see who's going to be the first one of us you talk to. It would be such an honor for me. Tod, will you talk to me first?"

"I'm talking to you right now," he said.

"I know! I can't believe it! I can't believe you're so nice. I had a dream about you and it was so real I thought maybe it actually happened to me. You were talking to me, the way you are now, just being nice, and you even held my hand." She looked around. "Why aren't they here now? They're never going to believe this. They'll think I'm making it up. Tod, would you do me a tremendous favor? Talk to me when I'm with my friends. Just walk by us casually and say, 'Oh, hi, Jen,' like you really know me. It wouldn't be a lie. You do know me now." They moved toward the gym. "I've got to go in here," she said. "Gym class. We're practicing for parents' night."

The Tod Ellerbee Fan Club! Ridiculous as it was, it gave him a lift. "So, you just want me to say, 'Hi, Jen,' and that's it?"

"That's all—we'll be outside after school." She pointed to the double glass doors. "Right there. It's got to be spontaneous, though. Remember, it's no good if I say, 'Hi, Tod,' first."

"Got it," he said.

She gave him a huge smile and went into the gym.

All afternoon he felt buoyant. Eighth period, he stopped in the biology lab to see Mrs. Pace. Last year, when he'd taken her advanced course in animal morphology, she'd talked to him about going into the natural sciences. She was the only one not enthusiastic about his going into law. "I don't see you as a lawyer," she said. "I don't think you're aggressive enough. You're smart, but you seem kind of hesitant sometimes, talking and so on."

That was why he'd taken Mr. Bodart's minicourse in public speaking. "Confidence," Mr. Bodart said every day. "Confidence is the key. Confidence! Say it to yourself, class. 'I have confidence.' Hold yourself confidently. Remember body language. Remember—*I have confidence!*"

Tod spent eight weeks in the class, but he didn't see much change in himself. It seemed useless to tell himself he had something he knew damn well he didn't have.

Now Mrs. Pace showed him a red-tailed hawk someone had shot and wounded. "I'm having trouble keeping him fed." She wore oversize glasses and her hair was chopped short. She was a no-nonsense person. She reached into the cage and stroked the hawk's feathers. "Mice are expensive, you better believe it. I can't afford them on my salary."

Tod thought he could trap some mice. "And rats, too, in the basement of the place where I work, Mrs. Pace."

He hung around for a while, helping her look for a three-foot-long water snake that had slipped out of its tank. They finally found it curled up in the wastebasket.

He was on his way home when he remembered Jen Kopp and the promise he'd made her. Yes, and the promise he'd made Amos. Two promises unkept. He ran back to school, but Jen wasn't anywhere around.

# 5

Saturday noon, before he went to work, Tod biked over to Carl's Automotive. Would Hilary Goodman be there? He didn't know, but it seemed easier to go someplace public such as a gas station than to ring her doorbell or phone her. Besides, he thought, justifying himself, there was that wobble in the front wheel that he could finally fix. The spokes probably only needed tightening, but he hadn't gotten around to it.

A convenience store selling milk, beer, and newspapers was attached to the garage. Tod locked his bike near the air pump and went in, trying not to look too directly at the girl behind the counter. She was sitting on a stool, turning the pages of a magazine. Nice enough looking, but something about her was a little spiritless. "Hi," he said.

"Hi," she said indifferently. Bangs down in her eyes and an armful of sizzling red and purple plastic bracelets.

There was a hot pretzel machine on the counter. "Could you give me change for a dollar for the machine?" Tod asked.

"Machine's not working." She yawned.

He bought a Million Dollar bar. He couldn't just stand there and stare at her, wondering what Amos saw in her. He handed her the dollar and she made change. "Have a nice day," she mumbled, and sat down again with the magazine.

He peeled the candy bar and ate it slowly, trying to figure out what to say next. He counted the cans of oil and antifreeze, then looked over the maps on the shelf. "Do you have a map of Hawaii?" It was a joke, but she didn't get it.

"Hawaii? I don't know."

A kid wearing a greasy cap and a blue mechanic's shirt with CARL'S AUTOMOTIVE lettered on the back came in from the garage and took a soda from the cooler. A tall, stoop-shouldered man came in after him. He was wearing an identical blue shirt. "Where'd you put the piston rings?" he asked.

"I didn't put them anywhere, Carl." The mechanic took a hasty swallow from the soda.

"Listen, Hil," Carl said in a weary voice, "were those rings delivered today or were they not?" The two of them went back into the garage.

Hil? *Hilary?* Tod turned to the girl behind the counter. "Can I ask you something? Is your name Hilary?"

She pointed toward the garage. "She works in there."

"In there?"

"That's what I said." She turned a page in her magazine.

In the garage, the mechanic—was it really Hilary Goodman?—was talking on the phone. "Carl says they were supposed to be here this morning, so what should I tell him?" When she got off the phone, she yelled, "Carl, they're coming this afternoon." She looked at Tod. "Yes?"

"Do you have a pressure gauge I could borrow?"

She pointed to a sign on the wall. WE LEND OUR TOOLS FREE BUT CHARGE FOR THE MECHANIC THAT GOES WITH THEM.

"I only want it for a second." He looked right into her face. Large gray eyes—nothing shy about them.

She opened a drawer and tossed him a gauge. "Don't forget where it came from."

"Do you happen to have a spoke tightener, too? I've got a wobbly front wheel."

"This isn't a bike shop," she said, but she went looking and found one. "You're lucky." She walked outside with him, turned the bike over, and spun the front wheel. "What'd you do to this wheel?"

"I ride it a lot. Close to a hundred miles a week." Was he trying to impress her? She started adjusting the spokes. "I can take care of that," he said, but she either didn't hear him or didn't want to hear him. She did the whole job, and when she was done, she asked Carl what she should charge him.

"Hourly rate," he yelled from inside, "the way we charge for anything."

Tod had to come up with ten bucks. He paid her and rode away without a word. When he looked back, she was watching him. "Okay?" she called, as if everything was terrific. That annoyed him, too.

Later, after work, he stopped at the store to see Amos and report that he'd broken the ice with Hilary Goodman. "So what did she say?" Amos opened a box of pale-yellow melons. "Does she know it's me? Vaccaro's Grocery store? The next time she comes in the store, I want you to be here with me, to keep me from getting too nervous."

"Slow down," Tod said. "I just met her. You can't rush these things. Why didn't you tell me she was a mechanic?"

"Isn't that fantastic? Isn't she beautiful?"

"Nice eyes," Tod said tactfully. He handed the melons to Amos one at a time. "This is the first step, Amos. The next step is we talk about you." Amos stood there, a rapt expression on his face. "And then it's up to you," Tod went on.

"You know what I dream about?" Amos raised a melon to his lips and kissed it. "Like that," he said, and he kissed it again.

All weekend that image of Amos's kissing the melon stayed with Tod. Wasn't it ironic that Amos had sent him on that errand to Hilary Goodman? Amos, for all his fears, was probably more at ease with girls than Tod.

Coming into school Monday morning, he saw Jen Kopp sitting on the stone wall with her friends. She had big satin bows on the ends of her braids. He shifted the paper bag he was carrying from one hand to the other. "Hi, Jen," he said.

She looked at her friends. "Oh! Tod! Hiii!" She hopped off the wall and walked away with him. "Did you see their faces? They died when you came over." She glanced at the bag he was carrying. "What've you got in there?"

"You don't want to know."

"Yes, I do, I'm curious about everything. What is it?"

"Something to eat."

"Is it a cake?"

"Hawk cake. Bird pie."

"Is that a puzzle? I hate puzzles. Let me see!" He opened the bag. Inside were three large rats in a home-

made cage. "Oh!" she said. "I never saw real rats before." She peered in. "They really do have ratty faces."

Everything about Jen was intense, the way she talked,
the way she used her hands and her eyes—even the
space she occupied seemed to buzz and hum.

They went up to the lab. Mrs. Pace wasn't there. The
hawk whistled when he sniffed the rats, a high flutelike
sound. "I'm sorry I forgot about Friday," Tod said, taking out a rat. "By the time I remembered, you were
gone."

"Oh, that's all right," Jen said. "This is *much* better."

They watched as the hawk held the rat down with
one claw and tore it apart with its beak. "Oh," Jen
breathed.

"Are you going to be sick?" he said.

She glanced up at him. "Never!" And she moved
closer to him.

# 6

"Hilary?" Tod said, squatting down. She was in the pit under a car.

She frowned up at him. "Hi, uh . . ."

"Wobbly wheel," he said. "Remember?"

"Oh, sure. More trouble?"

Outside, a dog started barking. *My friend sent me to talk to you. My friend Amos likes you. He wants you to give him a chance to get to know him.*

She came up, wiping her hands on a rag. "The bike is okay?"

"Yes, it's riding fine. Actually I didn't come in the other day to have my bike fixed." He couldn't resist adding, "I could have done it myself and saved ten bucks."

"Well," she said, "now you're telling me." She pulled her cap off and her hair spilled over her shoulders. He stared. There was so much hair. It was like a cape across her shoulders. "I thought you wanted me to do it," she said. "Why didn't you say something?"

"You took over—" he started, and then he stopped. "I didn't come here to talk about that." He tried a smile.

The dog was still barking, and Carl called over, "See what's wrong with Tanya, Hil."

Tod followed her outside. A large black and tan Doberman was up on its hind legs, in a small wire cage. "Tanya, what's the matter, girl?" Hilary said. "You lonely?"

"That cage is the trouble," Tod said. "That's no way to keep a dog, especially one her size." He reached into the cage to scratch her ears.

"Get your hands out of there," Hilary said. "She's a guard dog. Nobody handles her but Carl."

"Her collar's too tight," Tod said. "She needs water."

She gave him a who-asked-you look, but she went over to the spigot, filled an empty soda bottle, and then held it for the dog like a baby bottle.

"Not even a pan?" he said. "You'd be thirsty if you were out in the sun all day."

"Hey, back off," Hilary said. "It's not my dog. I'm only here part-time."

They were at the edge of an argument. "Sorry, Hilary," he said.

She gave him a suspicious glance. "How do you know my name?"

"I heard your boss . . ." A half-guilty smile crept over his face. Now didn't seem like the moment to mention Amos. She'd probably throw the bottle at him. He stroked Tanya's muzzle. "Oh, she's such a nice dog . . . yes, she is . . ."

When he looked around, Hilary was gone. He stayed with the dog a few more minutes. Congratulations, he told himself. You managed not to say one word about Amos.

Now that he knew who Hilary Goodman was, Tod saw her everywhere in school. He caught glimpses of her in the cafeteria, in the auditorium, in the halls. He caught her looking up at the moon. Looking at the moon! A paper moon that the Drama Club had hung in the cafeteria along with stars and rockets to advertise their new production. This moon-gazing Hilary was quite a different Hilary from the efficient mechanic. At least her clothes were different—jeans and a pink sweater—and her hair, loose and down to the middle of her back.

He followed her down the hall. When she stopped at her locker, he said, "Hi, remember me?"

She looked up. "How could I forget?" She shut the locker, tested it, and walked away.

*Amos, I tried,* Tod thought. *How about letting me off the hook?* But later, when he saw her in the parking lot, he tried again. She had her head under the hood of a green Mustang. He walked his bike past her. "Hi, Hilary." She looked up. Was that almost a smile?

That evening he called her from the bowling alley. "Hilary," he began. "How are you?"

"Great! Is this my cousin Donny?"

"Uh . . . no. It's Tod."

"Who?"

"Tod Ellerbee."

"Do you have the wrong number? This is—"

"I'm a friend of Amos Vaccaro."

"Who?" she said again.

"Vaccaro's Grocery store?"

"I don't think we ordered anything. Hold on a second, I'll check with my mother—" And she was gone. Tod hit his head against the wall.

"No, we didn't make an order," she said, coming back.

"Hilary, let me explain. I'm the wobbly wheel. The guy who petted Tanya."

"You're the tall blond guy?"

"Right, and you're the short girl with the greasy cap." There was a silence. "I didn't mean greasy exactly," he said.

"What did you mean?"

"It was just—I was surprised when I saw all that hair—"

"All that *hair*?" she repeated. "Surprised to find out I was a *real* girl, you mean?"

"Look, Hilary, I'm really botching this up. I apologize." Another silence, and he said, "I saw you today in the parking lot at school."

"No kidding. I saw you, too. So what's next?"

How was he going to get from here to Amos? He took a deep breath. "I'm getting off on the wrong foot with you," he began.

"Yes, you are." And that was it. He said something about seeing her in school next week and hung up. It was awkward.

# 7

Tod was in his room reading for his sociology class when he heard his father on the phone with Loretta, talking about her son. "Four hours ago?" his father was saying. "What are you so worried about? The hike and the fresh air will be good for Scott. . . . Okay, okay, I know it's not a joke. You want me to go look for him? Listen, if it makes you feel better—"

A few minutes later he was at Tod's door. "Feel like taking a ride?"

"Sure." Tod tossed his book aside.

In the car his father told him that Scott had gone horseback riding in Apple Valley. "He didn't want to go home when the other kids did, he told them he'd walk. Fine, but that was four hours ago. He hasn't called his mother, he didn't come home for supper, she has no idea where he is. If it was you who pulled that—"

"Don't tell me, Dad, I know. If it was me, you'd have turned over and gone back to sleep." His father had never hovered over him, even when Tod was small. He couldn't, of course, he had to work, and Tod had been

33

forced to become self-reliant. Most of the time he thought it was a good thing.

They drove all the way out to the stables. The buildings were dark, and the horses were inside. They walked around, calling Scott. The stable dogs started barking, and they went back to the car.

They drove slowly back to town watching both sides of the road, past miles of orchards, lines of ghostly trees with their chopped arms. Once a deer appeared, its emerald eyes gleaming out at them.

Loretta lived in the back apartment of a two-family house. The light was on, on the side porch. Loretta came to the door immediately. "You didn't find him? It's almost midnight!"

"We covered every inch of the road, Loretta," his father said. "Listen, he's fourteen—"

She ran down the steps and out to the street. "Oh, that boy!" She came back, and they stood around talking. "If you're going to wait," she said, "I'll go in and put on a pot of coffee." She'd hardly gone into the house when Scott came strolling around the corner.

"Look who's here," Tod's father said, and he went up on the porch to call Loretta.

"Where'd you come from?" Tod said. Scott was so damn casual. He sauntered along, drinking from a can of soda. "How'd you get back? Did you walk?"

"You wish, Ellerbee. I'm not that dumb." He was a big, heavy kid, a redhead. "I called somebody to come get me. A friend."

"I didn't know you had any of those."

"Aw, shut your mouth, Ellerbee. You make me sick."

What a punk, Tod thought. "We were looking for you."

Scott smirked. "You didn't look in the movies, did you?"

"Jerkhead! You could at least have called your mother." He shouldn't have said anything. Scott's smirk got broader. He was enjoying this.

Loretta came out on the porch. "Get in here," she said to Scott. She looked at Tod's father. "Thanks, Bob."

"What're you thanking him for?" Scott said.

"Shut up." She gave him a smart slap across the face, then followed him in and slammed the door.

"What a baby that kid is," Tod's father said on the way home. "I wouldn't trust him to open the door for me."

Tod sat there agreeing with his father, but in the back of his mind was another thought—a reproach to himself. Was he so mature? Look at this little thing he had to do for Amos—two weeks ago he'd promised to talk to Hilary Goodman about Amos, and what had he done since then except make a fool of himself in front of her?

The next time he saw her she was sitting alone at a table in the cafeteria. He went right up to her. Being decisive. None of this baby stuff. "Hilary Goodman," he said.

She looked up, but she didn't say anything.

"I have to talk to you about something." And he sat down next to her. "I don't mean to be mysterious, but there's this friend—" Then he hesitated. That was fatal. Were those gray eyes judging him? It was only a fraction of a second, but he lost ground. "I mean, do you think we could set up a time to talk?"

"What's wrong with right now?"

"Now?" Exactly what he'd wanted, but he began doing an Amos thing, clowning, pulling out his ID, his school cafeteria card with his picture on it, a real mug shot. "This is to prove who I am. If you look closely, you can even see a faint resemblance to the original."

"Not as bad as mine," she said, and produced her cafeteria card.

He looked at her. "Better in life. Much better."

"Oh, now I get it, you're selling something. What is it? Chocolates? Girl Scout cookies?"

"No, it's nothing like that." But in a sense he was selling, wasn't he? He was out to sell Amos. "I just wanted to talk to you about, well, about something I need to talk to you about." Now he sounded like an idiot. "I know this is off the wall," he said too loudly, "but would you ever consider going out with a guy from another school?"

"You mean a blind date?"

"I know, I know, that's a totally bizarre notion. You never go on blind dates, do you?"

"I never have," she said. "I haven't had that many dates."

"I can't believe that," he said, and he started clowning again, the spirit of Amos inhabiting him. "Just can't believe it, just can't belieeeve it."

"Believe it, believe it," she said. "How about you? Lots of dates, I bet."

"Me? Never. None."

"Oh, yeah, I bet." And she gave him that look he knew, the look of Leoni Cramer: *You good-looking guys!* Why couldn't girls look beyond the surface? Didn't they know that what you saw wasn't always what you got?

"My last date, my first date, was in tenth grade."

Stop, he told himself. This is self-pity, this is humiliation, this is unnecessary. What are you asking for, Tod? This is out and out begging. Stop, fool!

But there was something about the way she was looking at him, something in those gray eyes that kept him going. "This girl asked me out—Leoni Cramer, do you know her? No, you wouldn't, that was another school."

"You're new here?" Hilary said.

"My second year."

"This is my first."

"So we're both new." He paused and leaned on his elbow. Funny how finding out that someone else was in the same boat as you made you feel close to that person.

"So what about this Leoni?" she asked.

"Oh, she spent the whole evening telling me what a repulsive, revolting, uh, repulsive—"

"Repugnant?" she suggested.

"Yes—repugnant, disgusting—"

"Disagreeable?"

"Right. You got the idea."

"What a pathetic story, Tod Ellerbee."

So she did remember his name. "I have a lot of sad stories. Wait . . ." He went to the soda machine and bought two sodas. When he sat down again, he handed her one. "How'd you get interested in mechanics?" he said. He sat a little closer to her than he had before.

"I just always liked cars," she said. "I used to play with cars instead of dolls."

"Well, that's really—"

"If you're going to say *unusual*, don't. I've heard that all my life. Oh, it's so *unusual* to find a girl who likes motors. It's so *unusual* to see a girl who doesn't mind getting her hands dirty. It actually isn't that rare, but nobody stops to think about it. Everybody either wants to change me because I'm so *unusual* or pat me on the head for being so *unusual*. Ooogh!" She sipped her drink.

"I was only going to say it was interesting," he said. "I don't know much of anything about motors."

"Boy, *that* is unusual!" she said.

*Good, good, I'm getting things smooth so I can talk for Amos. Warming things up.* "There's something else I wanted to say about that blind date thing—" he began.

And she said, "I have something to tell you. I have a guilty conscience. I'm really sorry I had to charge you for fixing your bike."

"I was kind of sorry, myself," he said.

"But Carl pounds it into my head that people don't appreciate anything unless they pay for it. But straightening your wheel wasn't that much."

"Oh, it was good," he said. "You really fixed it, probably better than I would have done myself."

"What do you mean, *probably*?"

"Remember when I called you the other night, Hilary, and mentioned Amos Vaccaro?" He ran his finger around the rim of the soda can. "Well, that was a preliminary to—" God! Why was he talking this way? *A preliminary.* Why didn't he say what he meant? "Amos Vaccaro," he said, "is a friend of mine."

But then, instead of getting to the point, he started the story from the beginning, with the summer he was thirteen and jumped off the falls. He told her everything, even how hot it was that summer.

"So Amos saved your life."

"I've always felt that I owed him," Tod said.

"It's like the old Chinese saying, isn't it? That thing

that if someone saves your life—how does it go? If I saved your life, I'd be responsible for you forever."

"It's just the opposite for me," he said. "I feel responsible for Amos."

"It would work that way, too. It makes more sense actually."

A girl with her arms full of books sat down at the other end of the table. "How'd you do on the English quiz?" she called over to Hilary. The two of them began to discuss the test.

Tod sat back. Amazing how well he and Hilary understood each other. He liked her. It wasn't that she was pretty, although she was, it was her personality, the force of it—she was somebody, she had brains, she was down to earth, and if she said something, you listened. He'd never realized before what a great combination that was in a girl.

The sun came in through the long, dusty windows and fell across her hair. He remembered her taking off her cap at the garage and the way her hair had spilled over her shoulders. A feeling of gladness came up in him. A wonderful warm feeling made up of the sun, the nearly empty cafeteria, the scrubbed tables . . . and Hilary.

Hilary, he thought. Just that. *Hilary.*

"Tod! You there, man? You'll never guess who I talked to yesterday."

"Who?" Tod said.

"Hilary! She came by the store. She said, 'Hi, Amos.' She knew me, she knew me, Tod. You did it, man. I was outside, putting apples on the stand, and she stopped. I didn't even see her coming, and I was so surprised I spilled apples all over the sidewalk. She helped me pick them up. She said, 'Lucky they weren't eggs.' She's got a sense of humor. And you know what else? She knew my name.''

"You just said it."

"She said my name! She said, 'Hi, Amos!' What does that tell you? It tells me she knows me."

"I think you got something there."

"You bet I do! And you didn't hear the way she said it. It was great! I said, 'How'd you know my name?' She said, 'What do you mean, is your name a secret or something?' Then she said you were talking to her about me. She said you were a friend of hers."

Tod looked out the window. Beneath him, in the backyard, dignified, fat Mr. Mitchell was down on his hands and knees playing with his German shepherd. He and the dog were grinning at each other. "What'd she say exactly, Amos? I mean . . . about me."

"She said, 'Tod Bumblebee is—' "

"Amos, you're going to get killed."

"Okay, here it is straight. She said, 'I know Tod Ellerbee, he goes to my school, and he told me about you.' She said you told her I was a hero. Hey, man, what'd you tell her that for? I don't want her to think I'm a bragger, a lot of hot air. I'm not a hero. I didn't do anything great. I just did it. Right? How can I take credit for that? Tod, my mother's calling me, I gotta go. I just wanted to congratulate you for being a great friend. If you were here, I'd kiss you."

# 8

Paula! My sister, my nemesis. Nothing I do is ever good enough for her. She's always got to be superior. She came into my room while I was writing in my journal and asked me what I was scribbling. Typical. What she does is writing. What I do is scribbling.

And then when I told her—and why do I tell her anything!—that I was writing about a boy, she said, "Oh, the male sex. Nice. So, my little sister is normal, after all!" And she gave me an approving pat—I mean slap—on the head. Sometimes she acts more like ten years old than twenty. Still, talking about boys gave us something in common, and I told her about Tod. "What does he look like?" she asked. Trust Paula to go right to looks.

"Tall," I said. "Light blond hair. Cute eyes. Sort of like Sam Shepard, the actor, rugged like that."

"Wow," Paula said. "No wonder your face is all red. So it's puppy love!"

I got mad. "Please don't patronize me! Is it possible for you to understand that I could just be friends with a boy?"

"That's the kind of thing I worry about," she said, and she started in on me about working in the garage and what was *going to happen to me if I didn't get a little more feminine. "And don't tell me I'm behind the times, Hilary. I know women can do all kinds of things, but you've got a brain. I'd like to see you use it."*

*"You need brains to be a mechanic," I said. But she doesn't hear anything. She's never understood about me and cars and she's never tried to understand.*

*She wouldn't leave it alone. "Hilary, I'm not saying this to be cruel, but somebody has to tell you. Since you started working in that garage, you smell greasy. I smell grease right now on you."*

*I lost it then and started screaming. "You're a made-up, painted, intellectual phony! Get out of my room. And don't ever come back." But she had the last word.*

*"Bye bye," she said, and softly closed the door.*

*I opened the door and slammed it. Then I started sniffing my hands and my hair. I didn't smell anything but soap, but Paula got me agitated, just what she wanted.*

# 9

Tod was downtown on Gore Avenue, on his way to pay the electric bill, when he saw Hilary coming out of a store. She was wearing heels and big fan-shaped silver earrings. "Every time I see you, you look different," he said. He wanted to tell her how wonderful she looked. "I like your earrings."

"They're my mother's."

"But I miss your cap."

"My greasy cap?"

"Are you ever going to forgive me for that?"

"You're forgiven. . . . I just bought a birthday present for my sister." She showed him a leather-covered journal.

"Do you have just the one sister?"

"One's enough!"

"Any brothers?"

"No, but tons of cousins and aunts and uncles. Our family is huge on both sides. What about you?"

"Just my father and me," he said, and he felt a little flush of humiliation, as if he were confessing something shameful. How skimpy and insignificant that sounded.

They were like two dots, two specks in space. He did have grandparents in England and Houston, but he didn't know them. He didn't know any of his relatives.

He and Hilary walked around downtown together. Just like that they were together. It was so easy it amazed him. He stopped to pay the light bill, and then they bought a bag of hot roasted peanuts.

It was easy to talk to her. He told her about Scott, how he badgered his mother for money all the time. "Once he came into the bowling alley and took the money right out of the register."

"Stole it?" she said.

"Yeah, his mother had to fight with him to get it back. Every time I see this guy, I think of the sickening possibility that if my father and Loretta ever get married, Scott will be my stepbrother."

Suddenly Hilary stuck her hand under his nose. "Tell me something truthfully, does my hand smell? Do you smell oil or grease?"

He took her hand. If he'd more nerve, he would have kissed it. "I smell peanuts."

"No grease?"

"No grease."

She gave him a satisfied look.

They turned down a back street, and an odd thing happened—he looked up and saw Amos in a window above him. Or so he thought. He was looking at a large mural painted over an old brick wall. There were several of these murals downtown, part of a state project to beautify the city.

The mural in front of them was a picture of the street as it had been a hundred years ago: a lot of small stores with striped awnings and flags, women on the street in long dresses, and men in ties with garters on their sleeves. In an upstairs "window" above one of the stores, a girl leaned on a yellow pillow. And in the next window Tod saw "Amos" wearing a short red jacket and holding a trumpet in his hand.

It was Amos, or Amos's double, or Amos in another life. Amos's springy hair, Amos's eyes, looking directly at Tod. Looking hurt. Questioning. *Why? What about me? Why are you moving in on Hilary?*

"You want anything before we close up?" Loretta called over to Tod and Amos.

"We're going to bowl a few games," Tod said.

Amos chalked his fingers, then picked up the bowling ball. "So what's my next move with Hilary?" He stood looking down the alley with the ball cupped in his arm. It was late and they had the alleys to themselves. Amos rolled a spare.

Tod stood up to take his turn. *I did what you asked, Amos. I told Hilary about you. She's spoken to you. Now I want out.* He swung his arm and sent the ball down the middle. "Strike!" he called, but he was left with candlesticks. His next ball went right between them.

"I was thinking about calling her," Amos said, getting up. "But what do I say?"

"Amos, you don't have to ask me that."

Amos put his hand to his ear, holding an imaginary phone. "Hel-lo," he said in a deep voice. "Is this Hilary Goodperson? How'm I doing, Tod?"

"Terrific."

"No, I know I'm being stupid. Do you believe how scared I am? Scared I'm going to get tongue-tied. When was I ever tongue-tied?"

"Don't think about it so much. Just do it. Don't talk to me about it." Tod made an impatient gesture, but in his mind he saw a court, a judge, himself in the defendant's box. The crime he was accused of was disloyalty. Theft of affection.

*But Your Honor, I had no indication before the fact that this would happen. I didn't intend to like her. I didn't expect her to like me. This is not a case of premeditation or intent to harm. No criminal intent. My motives were pure. Events overtook me. Feelings and emotions beyond my control.*

The next time up, Tod caught only three pins. His concentration was shot. "Let's quit. I'm way off."

"Only two more frames. You can still pull it out. . . . Maybe I should take Hilary bowling. What do you think?"

"Ask her," Tod said roughly. "Don't keep asking me. Look, Amos, she knows you now, you've talked to her, you've broken the ice. Okay? Now, the rest is up to you. I am out of it."

"No, man, it's too soon. I still need moral support, I need advice, I need help with strategy."

"What is this strategy stuff? Is this a war? You've got a thing for a girl—"

"Not a *thing*, man." Amos sat down again with the ball in his lap. "I told you, I'm in love with this girl." No clowning now. No funny talk. No funny faces. "Maybe it's never happened to you, Tod, so you don't know what I'm talking about. A guy like you, someone who's got it all—looks, personality, the whole thing—you don't know what it means for someone like me."

"I don't want to hear any more of this," Tod broke in. "There's not one damn thing wrong with you. You've got a great personality and you don't need me to make a case for you with a girl you like."

He walked over to the counter and sat down. Amos joined him. "Can I get a tuna fish sandwich and pickles," Amos said to Loretta. He tore open a bag of potato chips.

Tod went behind the counter. "I'll make the sandwich, Loretta, you can close up."

"I know everything you tell me is for my own good," Amos said. "But you got to remember, man, this is all new to me. I'm asking you again, don't desert me."

Tod cut the sandwich in half. He didn't say anything. He didn't say yes, he didn't say no. It was the old thing: he couldn't refuse Amos. And the new thing: he couldn't tell him the truth, either . . . that he was in love with Hilary, too.

# 10

On Friday, a half day, Tod and Hilary went to his house for lunch. They were going downtown to the movies after they ate. Tod was a little anxious about her seeing where he lived. He wasn't ashamed of their apartment—it didn't smell, they washed their dishes and took out the garbage every day—but it wasn't a real home. It was just a couple of rooms.

"It's a place for me and my father to eat and sleep," Tod said dismissively.

"I like bare walls," she said. "It's restful. No junk to dust."

"You don't have to be polite."

"I'm not. That's what I think."

They sat around the kitchen, talking and eating corn chips and jam. "Do you remember the first comic book you ever owned?" she asked. He shook his head. "Spiderman," she said. "What was the name of your second-grade teacher?"

"I had three of them. Ms. Fishman, Mrs. Cobert, and—I forget the third one."

"My second-grade teacher was Mr. Rose. I remember he drove a big old white Caddy with fins."

"Do you remember buying goldfish?" he asked. "How about hamsters? Gerbils? Mice?"

After a while they went into his room. He got a music station on the radio. They sat down on the floor with their backs against the bed. "You want to hold my hand?" she said.

Yes, he wanted to hold her hand.

"Do you want to cuddle?" she said a moment later.

He smiled and moved closer.

And still later she said, "Do you want to kiss me?"

Did the sun rise in the east? Was grass green? Did birds fly?

They missed the early show but made the next one.

In the movies he watched her push fistfuls of popcorn into her mouth. Everything she did fascinated him. She brushed a strand of hair out of her face. She bit her lip when the hero on the screen fell into a pool of crocodiles. He watched her more than he watched the screen.

A few days later she invited him to supper. He imagined the two of them in the kitchen, standing around eating Chinese takeout. It wasn't anything like that. She had invited him to a formal sit-down meal with her whole family. There was a tablecloth, silver, glassware, even a centerpiece of flowers. Tod thought of the way he and his father ate at home with two plates, paper napkins, and the food in a pot between them.

He sat between Hilary's mother and her sister. He studied the place setting. Two spoons— one for dessert probably. A knife. Two forks. Which one to use first?

"So you're Tod," Paula said, and gave him a long, interested look. She was older than Hilary, but smaller and awfully pretty, he thought. She was wearing white overalls over a blue sweater. "I just bought these overalls, Tod. What do you think of them?"

"I'm not much of a fashion critic."

"Your basic male reaction is fine."

Hilary groaned. "Paula!"

"You don't think they're too pretentious?" Paula said. She was flirting with him.

"I didn't know overalls could be pretentious," he said. He saw Hilary's mother pick up the smaller fork for the salad.

"Do you go to Hilary's school, Tod?" Mrs. Goodman said. She was wearing a shawl and turquoise earrings.

"Yes. I graduate this year."

"Ah, to be in high school again," Paula said.

Hilary's father passed him the bread basket. "Tod, help yourself." He was bearded and blue-eyed. He asked Tod where he was thinking of going to college.

"Probably to State."

"What do you drive?" Paula said.

"A Peugeot."

"Oh! Mmm! Fantastic."

Hilary laughed out loud. "A two-wheel Peugeot, Paula."

"Oh, a motorcycle."

Tod shook his head. "No, a bicycle."

"But you're saving for a car," Paula said.

"No."

"You have to be! I never met a guy who didn't want a car."

"What does your father do, Tod?" Mrs. Goodman said. "Does your mother work?"

"Mom," Hilary complained, "Tod came here to eat, not answer a million questions."

"My mother's dead," Tod said. There was a little murmur of sympathy. "My father's an inspector on the line at Fairbanks." And then he mentioned that his father had been trained as an electrical engineer at RPI. He wasn't in the habit of giving out this information, or any information. Was he trying to impress Hilary's family? Her father was a professor of economics at the university.

"Why did your father give up engineering, Tod?" Professor Goodman asked.

Tod didn't quite know how to answer. He didn't want to get into the whole thing about his father's giving up everything after his mother died. "So I used to be an engineer," his father would say with a shrug. "So what will that and a dollar get you? Forget it, it's the past."

"Well . . . ," Tod said.

Hilary came to the rescue. "Maybe Tod's father is happier with what he's doing," she said.

"And why shouldn't he be?" her mother said, as if someone were disagreeing. "I'm a weaver," she said to Tod, "and I understand how people can get tired of computers and office work and want to do something real with their hands."

"Mom, now you're talking," Hilary said. "Listen to what you're saying! *Hands. Real work!*" She held up her hands. "Isn't that what I'm doing?"

"But college is important, too," her mother said. "A high school education is just the beginning, Hil. And don't forget Tod's father went to college before he made that decision."

They all started talking at once about Hilary's future. Tod sat back.

"Every educated person should be acquainted with the technology that surrounds us," Hilary's father said, banging the table with every word.

"Daddy, you've said that so many times. Don't be so stuffy. Just because I work in a garage doesn't mean I'm cutting off my education."

They were yelling at each other, they were loud, and Hilary was the loudest of all. "Why don't you guys let me make up my own mind? Let me make my own mistakes!"

After supper Hilary showed Tod around the house. "The five-cent tour," she said, pointing out the work her parents had done: the woodwork restored, the layers of paint removed. "My parents are fanatic for everything natural."

Tod tried to imagine living in a house like this, all these rooms, all this furniture, the front hall with its formal pier mirror, the winding staircase, the dark mahogany banister, the rugs and books and plants. Compared to this, he and his father were camping out.

On the second-floor landing, Hilary stopped in front of a narrow, old-fashioned desk with shelves on top and drawers underneath. "Isn't it beautiful?" she said. "It's going to be mine when I leave home. Nana left it to me."

"Hilary," her mother called up, "when you go up to your room—"

Hilary rolled her eyes. "I know, Mom. Door open and both feet on the floor." And then to Tod, "I used to hear her say that to Paula all the time."

Hilary's room was on the third floor. Tod went to a window and looked down on the street. What if Amos was out there, watching the house? What if he was looking up at Hilary's window? Tod stepped back, as if he'd been caught doing something forbidden.

"Tod, come here." Hilary showed him a bookcase full of model cars. "I built them all myself."

He picked up one of the cars. The doors, the hood, and the trunk all opened. When he reached inside, he could turn the steering wheel. "Clever little thing," he said.

"Me or the car?"

"Both."

They sat down on her desk, close, shoulders touching, and looked at her scrapbook. More cars. He thought about kissing her. "Did I tell you Amos couldn't swim when he rescued me? Can you imagine, that little guy—" He stopped. He shouldn't have said that, it was so patronizing. "He jumped in, he didn't hesitate."

Hilary put her hand over his. "You really love him, don't you? And he must love you, too." And she kissed him on the cheek, close to his mouth.

Then he kissed her on the mouth. She rubbed her forehead against his. And they kissed again.

When Paula came up later with a carton of vanilla ice cream and three spoons, they were sitting on the desk, swinging their legs like a couple of kids.

# 11

When the phone rang Friday evening, Tod was making himself a sandwich. "I just called Hilary," Amos announced. "I mean, I dialed, but then I got cold feet and hung up. I'm going to do it, though. Tonight I'm calling her."

"She's not home," Tod said. "She and her family went down to North Carolina yesterday to visit an eighty-year-old great aunt of hers."

There was a pause. "How do you know that?"

"I see her around school," Tod said quickly. Too quickly? "I talk to her," he said. *Talk to her? Come on, Tod, quit the bull!* He more than *talked* to Hilary and he more than *saw* her around school. Yesterday at lunch, which they'd eaten together, which they ate together almost every day, Hilary had told him about her family's travel plans. Their first separation. Four days! It was going to be four long days, he felt, and he wanted to say something to her about how much he would miss her, but he couldn't get it out.

"I wish I weren't going," she said. "I'm going to miss you."

"Really?"

"Yes, really!" She hit him on the arm. "Well?"

"What?" And then he got it. "Oh! Me, too!"

"So, do you talk about me?" Amos asked.

"Sure, what do you think?" Tod took a bite of his sandwich, then spit it out. Did he and Hilary talk about Amos? Yes. He could say that honestly, but he still felt like a crook. How could he explain to Amos what had happened? He couldn't.

All that cutesy, courtroom me-in-the-witness-chair stuff he'd come up with meant *zilch*. The point was that Amos had sent him on an errand—no, not an errand, a *mission:* he had trusted Tod to plead his case with Hilary. He had believed Tod would think of his interests, not Tod's own. And in fact, what had he done? Nothing for Amos. Everything for himself.

Could he say to Amos, *I didn't intend this to happen*!? It would be the truth, but what difference would that make to Amos? Was Amos then going to say, *No sweat, pal, if she likes you, that's great*!? And was Tod going to protest, *No, no, I'll step aside and give you your chance with Hilary*!? In a pig's eye, he would.

"Did she say how long she's going to be gone?" Amos said.

"I don't know," Tod stammered. Then, disgusted with himself, he added, "I think she said four days."

"Did she tell you anything else?" Amos said. "Am I sorry I didn't call her. I should have called her the other day. Four days? How'm I going to wait four more days?"

Suddenly, Tod imagined Amos and Hilary together in her car, Amos giving her one of those sympathetic, wanting looks of his. Amos letting Hilary know how much he was going to miss her. Amos torn up because he wasn't going to see her for four days—and telling her so. She wouldn't have to punch him in the arm to get him to say a warm, loving thing.

And then, in another trick of his mind, Tod heard Leoni Cramer's voice: *You and your cold, aloof face!*

Jen was waiting for Tod at his locker on Monday morning. "Tonight's the gym exhibition," she said. "Will you come and clap for me? My friends said I shouldn't ask you. They said it was really nervy of me, but I said if I wasn't nervy, you and I wouldn't even be talking." She had a way of tilting her head and peering up at him. "I'm right, aren't I?" she said.

"What time?" he asked. "Maybe I'll bring a friend of mine to clap for you, too." Amos and Jen, Tod said to himself. He liked both of them, they were bound to like each other.

"Who's that? A girl?" Jen said, frowning and tipping up her chin.

He tugged her braid. "You're jumping to conclusions. You'll see."

She put her hand over her heart. "Well, it would really hurt me if you were interested in other women. I suppose I have to expect it. You are an older man, and right now there's this big gap in our ages. But," she went on musingly, "in a few years, it won't seem like we're so far apart."

As soon as Tod got home, he called the Vacarros. Amy answered. Amos wasn't home. "You want him to call you, Tod?"

"As soon as you see him. Tell him it's important."

When Amos called later, Tod said, "Get dressed, we're stepping out tonight. This cute girl I know wants us both to come to her gym exhibition." If Amos and Jen liked each other—and why shouldn't they?—it would solve everything. They were nearer in age to each other. They were both outgoing and talkative and enthusiastic. How could they not like each other?

"This girl is really fantastic, Amos," he said. "She's got everything. I want you two to meet."

"I can't go out tonight, man, I'm working in the store. But what's her name?"

"Jen. Wait till you see her." Amos and Jen, he thought again. Even their names were perfect together.

"How long have you known this girl? Sly dog, how come I haven't heard about her till now?"

"No, no, no, you got it wrong," he said. "This isn't the girl I—" But he didn't finish. He didn't say—as he might have, as he should have to clear the air—*Hilary is the one, Amos. I'm sorry, but that's the way it is.*

He stayed on the phone too long with Amos, and he got to the gym only in time for the finale: everyone in formation to make the school initials, KHS, while the band played a brassy version of "Don't Rain on My Parade." Tod spotted Jen in the letter *K* and clasped his hands over his head, but he didn't think she saw him.

He waited for her near the locker room. "You did come!" Her face brightened. "Did you see me?"

"At the end, marching—I was late."

"You weren't here for the gymnastics part? Oh, that's okay." She was wearing a green dress with a big lacy white collar. "I didn't do half as well as I usually do. I'm actually glad you didn't see me. I had an off night." They walked outside. "I fell off the balance beam. I thought I was so psyched! I did start out completely confident, but my father didn't show up. I think that's what threw me off."

They walked toward her house. "When my parents divorced," Jen said, "they split everything fifty-fifty, including me. They almost sawed me in half. It was my father's turn tonight to be the proud parent." She looked away moodily. "They do not realize, either of them, how miserable they can make me."

They stopped under a light and Tod brought out his wallet and showed Jen his pictures. "Who's that girl?" she said.

"My mother. She died when I was three."

Jen looked at the picture of his mother for a long time. "She was beautiful." She looked at him and there were tears in her eyes. "You look just like her."

She stepped closer to him, her face tilted up. *Kiss me,* her face said. *Kiss me,* her lips said. *Kiss me,* her eyes demanded—or pleaded or argued. *You want to kiss me, I know you do,* they said.

He felt himself swaying toward her. How many kisses had he been offered in his life? Was there anybody sweeter than Jen? Was there ever a sweeter offer or a sweeter face?

Yes, he wanted to kiss her. Yes, yes, yes. But he walked away.

# 12

The day Hilary came back from North Carolina, she went home after school with Tod. They threw themselves down on his bed and started kissing. And then the phone rang. And rang. And rang. Until Tod answered it.

It was Amos. "Did you just walk in?" he said. "I just got home from school myself."

"I can't talk now," Tod said. He rubbed his eyes and yanked his hair, trying to clear his mind. He closed the door to his room, as if Amos could see through the wires, would know Hilary was in there.

"I just wanted to remind you about Saturday," Amos said.

"Right, right, I remember," Tod said, but he didn't know what Amos was talking about.

"Good! See you then."

It wasn't until the next day, walking home from work, that Tod remembered Saturday was closing day of the State Fair. Every year he and Amos went together.

A car stopped. "Need a ride?" It was Hilary's sister, Paula.

"Thanks." He got in next to her. They didn't say

59

anything for a while. Then he said, "You going to the State Fair Saturday?"

She gave him an amused look. "Never! That pig-out!"

"It's fun," he said a little defensively. "The animals are great."

"There isn't anybody in our family who ever goes," she said.

That's when he decided he was inviting Hilary to the fair with him and Amos.

At home, Loretta and his father were in the living room playing cards. "Hey, guys," he said. They both looked up and smiled.

"Hi, kiddo," Loretta said.

"What have you been up to?" his father said. "Sit down, sit down."

Tod talked to them for a while, then went into the kitchen to get something to eat. He could hear them laughing in the other room. He went out on the back porch and fed the rabbit the rest of the spaghetti. "So what have you been up to?" What did it take to make a rabbit happy? A little grass, a girl rabbit . . . What did it take to make *him* happy? He was happy, but . . . but what? But what about Amos? He put the rabbit back in the cage and shut the door. If only Amos would forget Hilary. Find another girl. Ask Tod to do something else for him. Anything else. He only had to name his wish.

Late Saturday afternoon Tod and Hilary drove over to the store to pick up Amos. Hilary waited in the car while Tod went in. He hadn't told Amos that she was coming. Amos was behind the cash register, but he was dressed to go, white shirt and white pants.

As soon as he saw Tod, he yelled, "Amy, up front!"

And then to Tod, "The poor man's intercom. . . . Amy, step on it," he bellowed again.

His sister came ambling out from the back. "You ready to go?" She put down the bagel she was eating. "'Hi, Tod!" She whistled. "Look at my brother. Sometimes I can't believe we're twins. He's gorgeous, isn't he?"

"Cut it out," Amos said, looking pleased.

She adjusted his collar. "Women, look out, here comes my brother."

"We'll get the fair bus downtown, okay?" Amos said as they walked out. He stopped and looked at Hilary's green Mustang. He shaded his eyes. "Is that *Hilary's* car?"

"Yeah, I thought we'd all go together," Tod said, as if it had been the most casual thought. And it had started that way, but by now there was nothing casual about it. Tod wanted Amos to see Hilary and him together. He wanted Amos to see the way things really were. He wanted Amos to figure things out for himself without Tod's having to say anything.

"Is that really Hilary?"

"That's her. I invited her."

For a moment they were like the three points of a triangle—Amos and Tod side by side and Hilary in the car. No, Tod thought, not a triangle. It wasn't Hilary and Amos and Tod. It wasn't the three of them. It was Hilary and Tod. *Hilary and Tod!* A straight line from Hilary to Tod and from Tod to Hilary.

"My man!" Amos turned to Tod. "Wow!" He gave Tod a terrific smile. "You arranged this," he said. He was astounded. "You did this for me. Tod! You are a saint. You are the greatest friend." Then, before Tod could say anything, Amos ran back into the store.

Tod went down to the car and smiling, leaned into the window toward Hilary. He didn't feel like smiling. He felt queasy, deceptive. He wished he'd told her everything. He wished he'd told Amos everything. He wished this day were over with. "Hil, there's something I never told you," he began.

"Where'd Amos go?" she said, peering around him.

And just then Amos came running out of the store holding a tin of cookies over his head like a trophy. He stepped—almost pranced—to the car. "Hello, Hilary! Hello! Hello!" He opened the door and sat down in the bucket seat, then jumped out and held the seat down. "Get in, Tod," he said, bowing him into the backseat.

Tod almost burst out laughing. *Him* in the backseat? Amos wasn't getting the message. It was Tod and Hilary. He looked hard at Amos. "Youth before age," he said. "You get in first."

"No, no. Beauty before youth," Amos said. "Good-looking son of a gun, isn't he?" he said to Hilary. In the end, it was Amos in the front seat and Tod in the back.

Hilary glanced back at Tod. He raised his shoulders and gave her a wan smile. St. Ellerbee? St. Dope was more like it. He spent the whole ride to the fair staring glumly out the window, while Amos carried on with Hilary.

First it was the cookies. Amos couldn't say enough about them. "Danish butter cookies for you," he said to Hilary. "Top of the line. Do you like them? You have to like them, they're the finest cookies you can beg, borrow, or steal."

He was in top form. Jokes and stories tumbled out, one after the other. "Listen, I gotta tell you this, it's a classic Amos story." And he told Hilary how he'd run for president of his class. "Guess what my platform was, Hilary. Two words. *Trust Amos*. I thought that said it all. I didn't make any speeches. No posters. That was it. You know what I handed out?"

"Pens with your name on them?"

"McIntosh apples. Ask me why."

Hilary laughed. "Why?"

"Because my father got a truckload at the farmers' market."

Hilary drove with just the tops of her fingers on the wheel. "So how many votes did you get?"

"Three. . . . No, no, I'm just kidding you. I lost, but I came in second. Don't ask me how many candidates there were." And he laughed harder than Hilary.

⁕Amos turned around and passed the cookies back to Tod. Tod shook his head. "Take some," Amos urged. "That's an eight-ninety-five tin, imported butter cookies from Denmark." He kept urging the cookies on Tod, and Tod kept shaking his head. There they were, he thought, Hilary and Amos up front like the mommy and the daddy, and here he was, like the sulky kid in the backseat. And he was sick of it. At the fairgrounds he got between Hilary and Amos. Enough was enough.

He took Hilary's arm, he did more than that—he took charge. He had their agenda worked out. "First we take pictures," he said. He wanted a picture of Hilary and him, but Amos squeezed in with them in the booth. So what they got was a picture of the three of them, Tod and Hilary next to each other with Amos's chin resting on Tod's shoulder.

Agricultural machinery was next. "This is for Hilary," Tod said.

"Oh, great!" She held his arm.

*Do you see what's going on, Amos? Do you see the way we are with each other? Do you see the way I am with her? I know this girl! I know what she likes.*

Hilary was in her glory at the exhibit. She had questions for all the salesmen. She climbed up into the cab of a monster tractor and waved down to them.

*Do you see her, Amos? Do you know how passionate she is about machines? No, you don't! But I do.*

"Animal barns next," Tod announced.

"Oh, I know who this is for." Amos rolled his eyes at Hilary, and seeing the roosters, he crowed and flapped his arms. The roosters were as big as dogs, with brilliant red combs. Every time one crowed, Amos crowed along with it.

Tod steered them to the workhorses next, the Belgians and Clydesdales with their heavy hooves and big, warm, threatening bodies. *"Equus caballus,"* he said, showing off for Hilary. He was keyed up. He held her arm possessively. "Inhale!" he ordered. "Horse dung is one of the great smells of the world."

"Yeaagggh." Hilary grabbed her throat, and Amos gagged, and then the two of them slapped their palms together. Later, looking back, Tod identified that moment as the moment he began to lose control: lose his authority and his confidence and his connection to Hilary. He had tried to orchestrate the whole scene, he was the conductor, but suddenly the horns went wild, the instruments revolted.

"I want to see the goats," Amos said.

"Goats are insignificant and boring," Tod said.

"Okay, you commune with the horse dung," Hilary said. "We'll meet you by the door." And she and Amos walked off together.

He stood there. What did he care about horses? Without Hilary, the whole fair went flat. He waited long enough so they wouldn't think he was running after them, then he joined them.

Later they got hungry. "What'll it be, folks?" Amos said. "Chicken wings? Fried skins? Hero sandwiches? It's on me." He did a little tap dance and went off to stand in line.

"The guy is skinny, but he's always hungry," Tod said.

"He's so much fun to be with," Hilary said.

Which wasn't exactly what Tod had in mind. Nor was anything that happened after that what he'd intended. They sat down at a table with the food, Hilary between them, and suddenly he understood clearly that he and Amos were in a competition, both of them vying for her attention.

"Is the food okay?" Amos said. "Did I bring enough? You want ketchup, Hilary? Mayonnaise? Mustard? Extra onions? Just snap your fingers."

"I'm fine, I'm fine. Sit down, you nut."

Tod ate glumly. Was he fun to be with? He didn't feel like much fun right now. He didn't know how to put on an act for Hilary. He didn't wait on her with adoring looks. He adored her, all right, but he didn't know how to show it.

Amos bounced up to get Hilary a fresh napkin. He produced a straw for her drink, offered her the rest of his chips. "Anything else you want, Hilary, anything you need, just ask."

Tod sat back, his arms crossed, studying Amos. It was as if Amos was parodying Tod's pledge to him, poking fun at the words that had bound them together. *If you ever want, if you ever need . . .*

On the midway, Amos eyed a giant blue teddy bear, the prize in a ball toss game. "Three balls for a dollar," the barker cried.

Amos handed her five dollars. "Stand back, everyone." He made a production of it, naturally. He drew his arm back, wound up, and threw. And missed. And missed. And missed. And missed three more times.

"It's fixed," Tod said. "Come on, Amos, don't waste your money."

"Watch this," he said. "One more." And he won.

The teddy bear was for Hilary. "Oh, he's sweet!" She hugged it.

Amos gave Tod a blissful, contented look that was like a knife in Tod's heart.

The rides were next. Hilary went straight for the cars, of course. They got into separate cars. Tod concentrated on whacking into Amos.

"Help, Hilary!" Amos called. The two of them went after Tod.

"I have never had so much fun in my life," Hilary said when they got off. "I want to go on the Ferris wheel."

"Me, too!" Amos said.

Tod, like a fool, said that was too tame for him. So he was left holding the stupid teddy bear and watching them come around, hanging on each other and screaming. They came off the ride glowing. "You should have come, Tod," Hilary said. She took back the teddy bear and kissed it. "Teddy Blue, did you miss me?"

A woman turned and smiled at them, at Amos and Hilary. They looked good together, Tod thought. Wasn't there something heartwarming, something especially appealing about a short guy and a taller girl? Or maybe it was something about the two of them in particular—Amos with his dark face, dressed all in white, and Hilary with the sleeves of her sweater pushed up and her long, crinkly hair falling in her face.

After that, everything went steadily downhill. It was no longer even a question of Tod's showing Amos the way things *really were*. If it was anybody's show, it was Amos's. He was the master of ceremonies, and Hilary was both the audience he was charming and the star he praised. And the more charming and entertaining Amos became, the more inept and distant and cut off Tod felt.

They stopped to watch Bozo, the clown with the dirty mouth. He sat in a cage, perched on a narrow seat balanced over a tank of water. The trick was to hit the target and knock the clown into the water. Bozo's speciality was insulting people until they got mad enough to toss down a dollar for a ball. "Hey, fatso," he said to a man with a potbelly, "when's the baby due?" The crowd laughed. "Toothpick," he said to a thin woman, "if they turned you sideways, you'd disappear." The man with her grabbed a ball and hit the bull's-eye.

Bozo came out of the tank, spitting water and talking. "Big ears!" He looked straight at Tod. "Yeah, you, the long one with the rabbit ears."

Tod couldn't help glancing at Hilary and then at Amos, whose small ears were pinned neatly against his head.

"Was your mother an elephant?" Bozo yelled.

Tod dropped a dollar and threw the ball. It bounced off the cage. Bozo clapped. "That's the way. Your ears are still big enough to land planes on."

"Shut up!" Tod yelled.

"Hey, man," Amos said, giving Tod's arm a shake.

"Don't *man* me!"

Amos and Hilary glanced at each other. Something seemed to pass between them, a message, an understanding, as if they were the pair and Tod was the one on the outside, the one they felt sorry for.

"Come on," Hilary said, taking his arm. "That Bozo is an idiot."

He could barely stand her touch. He was in a rage of humiliation. He couldn't stand pity. He shook her off and walked away.

Hilary started after him. "Tod?"

"Forget it! Forget it!" He pushed through the crowd, saw things in a blur. A group of guys wearing purple pants . . . a boy in a studded jacket and girls with pink hair floating over their heads like cotton candy. He knocked into someone and kept going. A guy with muscles like iron balloons walked toward him, his sleeveless yellow T-shirt proclaiming, I WAS BORN AN ANIMAL. WHAT'S YOUR EXCUSE?

"Easy, brother," he said to Tod. Tod glared, ready for a fight, ready to beat someone up or be beaten up: either way would have satisfied the misery in him.

# 13

His father and the landlord were sitting at the table when Tod got up. They were drinking coffee and talking about their wars. His father's war was Vietnam. Mr. Mitchell's was the "Big One," World War Two.

"Here he is at last," his father said. "You know what time it is?"

"What time?" Tod rubbed the sleep out of his face.

"It's almost noon. What were you going to do, sleep the day away?"

Tod poured himself a cup of coffee. After yesterday he hadn't even wanted to get out of bed. His father was talking about his friend, Richie Gribble, the one who had died in Vietnam. He always said the same things about Richie. "We grew up together in Sacramento, we went right through school together, we did everything together, even enlisted together, right out of high school. We thought it was going to be a picnic. That shows you what a couple of dumb kids we were."

"Did I get any calls?" Tod interrupted.

"If you were in the service," Mr. Mitchell said, "you'd be up at four-thirty, Tod. And if you were in combat,

69

forget sleeping. When I was in the Battle of the Bulge—"
He paused. "You ever hear about that one?"

"Don't ask my son about the Battle of the Bulge,
Mitch. He thinks it's some kind of diet."

Tod took a doughnut. Hard to believe that Mr. Mitchell, who looked like a pillow tied in the middle, had ever
been a soldier.

Tod sat down. Should he call Hilary? He hadn't
called her last night, and she hadn't called him. He wanted
to call her, he wanted to hear her voice, he wanted to
hear her say everything was okay, everything was just
the way it had been between them before the fair. He
wanted them to laugh together about Amos's showing
off for her and his own fit of jealousy. *Yeah,* he'd say, *I
acted like a first-class jerk yesterday. I blew it, Hilary. Did you
notice I wasn't my usual charming self?*

"Kids don't know anything these days," his father
was saying. "You know what I heard, Mitch? Ninety
percent of kids don't know Mexico is our southern
neighbor."

Tod chewed his doughnut moodily. It was stale.

"Tod," his father said, "Mr. Mitchell is going to
electrify the garage. I told him you'd dig the ditch for the
underground service."

Was his father being funny? "These doughnuts are
stale, Dad!" He tossed it into the sink.

Mr. Mitchell's hands went to his back. "I'd do it
myself, but this back of mine—"

"Mitch, don't say a word," Bob said. "You don't
even want to think about it. My boy'll do it."

Tod put his cup down. *Tod will do it?* Sure, friendly
Tod! Do you want a ditch dug? Ask Tod. You're looking
for a girlfriend? Ask Tod.

"Get dressed," his father didn't let up. "If you get going on the digging now, you'll have it done in a couple hours."

"Dad . . ."

"Don't *Dad* me. Just get going!"

His insistence finally alerted Tod that his father was in the *up* stage of one of his down moods. First he went up, up, up, and then he went down, down, down. When he was up, he did ten things at once, and when he was down . . . Tod didn't even want to think about it.

He stood up. "Sorry, Mr. Mitchell, I've got to work this afternoon."

"You got plenty of time," his father said. "When do you go to work, four o'clock? Come on, I'll work with you. It won't take us an hour to get that little sucker done. Let's show Mitch what a couple of Ellerbee men can do when they put their minds to it."

"You mean their backs," Tod said.

"He's got his father's sense of humor, Mitch. Get dressed, Tod, I'll pour you another cup of coffee. And put on a pair of boots."

When Tod came out of his bedroom, he said, "I'm going out, Dad." He had his sneakers on, and he went straight to the door. "If anybody calls me, tell them I'll be back later."

"Hey," his father said, "where you going? What have you got to do that won't wait an hour? What's the matter? You got a girlfriend now?"

"Shut up," Tod said, and slammed out.

At work, Tod couldn't concentrate on anything. He tried to stay out of Loretta's way. She was in a foul mood, too. Maybe because her big, babyish son was following her around, begging for the car.

Tod tuned them both out. For some reason all he could seem to think about was his father's friend Richie.

In the picture on his father's bureau, they had their arms around each other. "I really loved that guy," his father would say. "Richie . . . when I lost him, it was like I lost my right arm. You don't find friends like that too often." And after Amos saved Tod's life, his father would always add, "Just like you and your friend Amos."

Yeah, sure. His friend Amos. What friend? He was going to lose Amos, wasn't he? If it was going to be Hilary and Amos, that was it. He couldn't be friends with Amos after that. Or Hilary, either. Oh, was he feeling sorry for himself! Poor, lousy orphan. He'd lost his mother, his father hated him, and the only two other people he'd ever loved were walking right out of his life with their arms around each other.

"You going to vacuum today or not?" Loretta said, walking by Tod with a tray full of empty bottles. "It helps if you turn on the machine." Then she turned to her son, who was hovering behind her. "And you! Will you stop following me, Scottie, and do something useful? I want those windows washed."

"They're not dirty."

"I'll decide that."

"If I can't have the car, I'm not doing anything," Scott said.

"Well, then just get out from under my feet. I have work to do here."

"You act like this is your home," Scott said sullenly.

"It puts food on the table and gas in the car, doesn't it?" She waved to some people who'd just come in.

"Mike, you and Donna take alley six," she called. She knew everyone who came into the place.

"Give me one good reason why I can't have the car, Ma," Scott said. "One good reason, then I'll leave you alone."

"You're only fourteen. You only have a learner's permit. That's two reasons."

"I won't hurt the goddamn car!"

"You can't have the car. No. Period."

Tod turned on the vacuum cleaner and drowned them both out.

When he came home after work, his father was on the couch, his feet up. Bad sign. He was wearing his GI fatigue cap. Another bad sign.

The TV was on. Tod watched for a minute. Willie Randolph was on first, threatening to steal second. On the split screen you could watch Willie and the pitcher at the same time. Willie took three steps, then leaned toward second. The pitcher whipped around and threw to the first baseman. Willie dove safely in under the ball. Three more times the pitcher did it, and three more times Willie dove under the ball.

"Anybody call me?" Tod asked.

No answer.

"Did the phone ring today, Robert?" His father stared at the screen. Tod felt anger coming from his father, rising off his skin like the smell of the cigarettes he was smoking. "Hey, I'm sorry I told you to shut up, Dad. I apologize. You want me to do some digging on that ditch now?"

"Sure, I'll get the flashlight. . . . It's done. I did it."

"You did it?"

"Yeah. I did it. Did you think I was going to wait for you?"

"What are you, pissed or something?"

No answer.

Another big baby, Tod thought. He went into his room. He was just sitting there in the dark, thinking, when the phone started ringing. He was thinking about him and his father, how they looked at things from opposite poles. His father was cynical, detached, he didn't want anything, he didn't believe in anything. And he, Tod, wanted everything. He wanted Hilary, he wanted . . .

"Get the phone," his father yelled.

He answered, hoping it was Hilary. "Tod, is the man in?" Loretta said.

"Wait a second, Loretta." He went into the living room. "It's Loretta," he said.

"'Tell her I'm not here."

"Why?"

"Because I don't want to talk to her."

"Then tell her yourself."

His father switched channels.

In the kitchen Tod picked up the phone. "Loretta? I don't see him anywhere around. Maybe he went out to get some beer or cigarettes."

"Oh." A pained little silence. Tod hated this, hated lying for his father. "I'm home now," she said. "I thought he was coming over. Well, tell him I called."

"Will do." He hung up. "Bob," he yelled. "Bob!" He went into the living room and stood over his father. "I did your dirty work. You could at least say thanks."

His father raised his cap and tipped it mockingly at Tod. Then he swung his feet to the floor, brushed past him, and went out.

*Him and his damn moods. Where's he running to now?*

*The next step will be giving up the apartment and moving
again. Like hell. If he does that, I'm not going.*

He went out on the back porch and started cleaning
the rabbit's cage. He heard the Mitchells downstairs,
talking. There were lights on in the neighborhood. All
around him, people were together in their homes, eating,
talking, watching TV, getting along, doing things together.

He heard someone coming up the back stairs. He
looked up. "Dad?"

Amos's head appeared. "Just me!" He stopped on
the steps and stood there, grinning. "Where'd you go
yesterday, man? One minute you were there, the next
minute you're gone." He came up on the porch. "Hildy
and I looked everywhere for you."

*Hildy?* Tod folded fresh papers for the cage.

"How'd you get home? Hildy and me—we thought
about leaving, too, but we weren't sure if you were just
being sick in the bathroom or something. I went and
checked. Did you meet somebody? You should have hung
around. Man, we had a wild time. That Hildy is something else."

Tod's ears, those damned elephant ears, were burn-
ing. He couldn't stand the way Amos was talking. Every
other word was "Hildy." It was "Hildy," and then a
sigh. And Hildy drove them home, and they sat in Hildy's
car, and Hildy this and Hildy that. It maddened Tod.
"Hildy? You call her *Hildy*?" The words came out like
steam escaping from a boiling pot.

"My pet name for her," Amos said proudly.

Tod shoved the soiled papers into a plastic bag, spit,
then grabbed a broom. "Move over."

Amos hopped up on the railing. "Man, you're a
grouch." He sat back and started humming.

"What's the point, Amos?"

"What, man? The point of what?"

"This visit! What's the point!" He was aware that he was acting like his father, and that made him feel nastier than ever. "What'd you come over here for?"

"Oh, you know . . . well . . . *you know.* I thought you'd want to know. We were in her car and—"

"I don't want to know about it," Tod said. "I don't want to hear your bull." He remembered himself at fifteen, horny, horny every minute. He had devoured girls with his eyes. He dreamt he could see through their clothes. He wanted their bodies. But—Hilary wouldn't. . . . No, not with Amos. No.

"She's too old for you," he said.

"What's age mean, man? You said it yourself, remember?"

"I'm telling you, you're too young for her. You're just a—" He caught himself.

"I'm gone over her," Amos said. "I don't want to do anything wrong. Should I just—"

*Just shut up, Amos. Do whatever the hell you're going to do and leave me alone.* Tod picked up the rabbit in the cage and slung it on his shoulder. He started down the stairs. Amos followed.

"You should meet another girl," Tod said, over his shoulder. Was there only one girl in the world? Why Hilary?

"What for? Are you kidding? Hildy's the only girl for me." His voice softened. "I'm telling you I love her. I mean it, Tod, this is it, this is eternal. Where're you going, man? What're you doing with that cage?"

"Taking a walk."

"With the rabbit?"

Tod stopped near the railroad tracks, away from houses, and let the rabbit out of the cage. It crouched near his foot. A crow flew overhead, and the rabbit's ears stiffened.

"You got him tamed," Amos said, and just then the rabbit sprang into the underbrush. "Hey! You want to get him back?"

Tod picked up the cage and turned toward home. The rabbit was free now. Maybe he'd survive, maybe he wouldn't. He was on his own. Like Amos, Tod thought. Like himself. Like Hilary. Like his father and Loretta. Like everyone. *We're all on our own*, he thought. *All of us, alone.*

# 14

*I saw Tod in school. He nodded at me and kept going, didn't even give me a chance to say hello. How can he do that? How can he look at me and just keep going? What's happened? I don't understand. Who needs this? Who needs a guy like that? My life was okay before he came around with his soulful eyes and his wobbly bike wheel!*

*Give me someone like Amos, who's cheerful and funny and makes you laugh. For once Paula's right in her advice. She says find a guy who'll make you laugh and you'll never go wrong.*

*Amos doesn't stand on his dignity, and I like him for that. I respect him. He's not all tied up in knots like Tod.*

*The guys in my old school put me down as a girl greaser. And to me they were goody-goody suburban types. So I came here to this school, expecting nothing from guys. Just leave me alone. And instead, I met Tod. I couldn't believe my luck. . . .*

*And now this. All week he hasn't called me. Damn him! He can go to hell. Let him run away. Let him do whatever he wants to do. I'm not going to stop him. I'm not going to chase him.*

*Forget Tod. Forget him. I wake up in the morning, look out my window at the trees. I love the trees. Then I think of* him. Forget him. *Then I go to school and I'm looking for him. In the corridors, in the lunch room. I pretend I'm not doing it, but I am.*

*I don't understand him, I'll never understand.*

# 15

Tod had gotten himself into a situation he didn't know how to get out of, and it made him miserable. And ugly. Gave him ugly thoughts. In school he searched for Hilary, but when he saw her, his face tightened and he turned away. At home he holed up in his room.

"How come you're so friendly?" his father said one night. "I haven't seen you smile for days. Can't stand a little fight with the old man?"

"It's got nothing to do with you," Tod said.

"Girl trouble?"

"None of your business." Tod studied the pattern on the wallpaper: little blue sailboats with red trim. It had been there when they moved in.

"Don't let the women get you down," his father said.

"You know all about it, don't you?"

His father took a drag on his cigarette. "I'll ignore the sarcasm. And, yes, I know quite a bit about it, and if you want my advice—"

"I don't."

"—for what it's worth—"

"Nothing to me," Tod said. "I'm not a tomcat."

His father's fist went up and so did Tod's. They stared at each other, bristling like a couple of apes. Then his father gave a little laugh. "Big shot," he said, and walked out. Tod's heart pounded. He'd never raised his fist to his father before.

At work Loretta noticed his moodiness. "You want to talk?" She patted her shoulder. "Come on, we can cry together."

That got a smile out of him, plus a little guilty fantasy: Loretta in his arms, Tod comforting her, stroking her . . . He said something about getting behind in his schoolwork, that he might fail trig. "I might not even graduate." The way he felt, it seemed possible at that moment.

"Fail?" Loretta pushed up the sleeves of her sweater. "Sit," she ordered, as if she were talking to Scott. "Someone's got to talk sense to you, Tod. That's a dumb thing you just said. You're too smart to fail."

He glanced furtively at her long, smooth arms. "Even if I don't fail, I don't have the money to make it all the way through college."

"Oh, come on, Bob is going to come through for you." *Yeah? The way he comes through for you?*

She opened a can of soda and put it in front of him. "I know there are loans and scholarships. Are you saving your money? I want you to save your money."

He nodded meekly. He liked her lecturing him.

"Well," she said, "at least it's a pleasure to give hell to someone who doesn't mouth off at me."

To torture himself Tod went up Highland Avenue, past Hilary's house. The attic windows were dark. Was she up there in the dark, with Amos? He got away from there, turned one corner and then another.

Downtown he walked into a McDonald's. What a mistake. It was a sad, dismal place. All the kids working behind the counter had swollen, pimply faces. The few people sitting there were old and worn-out. And Tod sat there too, eating a tasteless fish sandwich, too depressed even to leave.

In school the next day he saw Hilary at an assembly. He stared at her, willing her to turn and look at him. And she did. It was eerie. She looked straight at him. He half rose in his seat. *Hilary!* Everything came up into his throat. The words were there. *Why aren't we together? I miss you. I'm sorry. I've been a fool. . . .* She looked at him, saw him, and turned away.

In the cafeteria later, the noise was like ten jets taking off. Tod pulled a chair over to one of the windows. He put his feet up on the heat register and read and reread the same paragraph on the causes of the Civil War.

Were he and Hilary at war? When had the first shot been fired? Was his first small defeat when he let Amos take the front seat in her car? If he was at war with Hilary, wasn't it time for a truce? He was ready to fly the white flag. He'd carry it into school, wave it in the halls, hold it up in the cafeteria. *I surrender, Hilary. You win.* But what did she win? Amos? Him? Both of them?

Cool hands covered his eyes. "Hello," Jen breathed in his ear. He smelled spearmint gum. She sat down next to him and studied Tod's face. "You look like you have a black cloud over your head."

He put a straw in his book for a place marker. "Yeah."

"'Yeah what? You can tell me. It's a girl, isn't it?" Her eyes filled.

He rubbed her arm and remembered that moment in front of her house, her face tilted toward his. If only Amos and Jen liked each other. Yes, that thought again. Amos and Jen . . . and Hilary and Tod. They'd each have someone and everyone would be happy.

"Is she the one I see you with?" Jen asked. "What's her name?"

"*Saw* me with," he corrected. "You don't see us together anymore. Her name is Hilary." And then it all came out, the whole story—more, much more than he'd intended. "So that's the way things are," he concluded gloomily, and looking into Jen's sympathetic eyes, he felt the self-pity rising again in him. "Oh, well," he said, trying to sound brave, "that's the way the ball bounces." But then, almost desperately, he said, "Jen, what do you think I should do?"

"It's not an easy case," she said. "It's complicated. As I see it, there are two parts to it. Part one is that you didn't tell Hilary you met her because of Amos. And part two is that you didn't tell Amos the way you feel about Hilary. Tod, if it was you and me and you did that to me, brought in this other guy and sort of dumped him on me—"

"I didn't dump him on her, Jen. What I wanted was to make everything clear. I wanted Amos to open his eyes and see the way things were without me having to spell it out. I thought it would be kinder that way."

"Well," she said, "you didn't go about it right. I don't agree with you. You should have told Amos. Just been frank. And you should tell Hilary now."

"You think so?"

"If it was me, and you told me and explained everything, I'd understand. And something else, Tod. If you were so truthful, it would only increase my admiration for you. I mean, that's really selfless of you, giving up your girlfriend to another guy."

"I told you, I didn't give her up, Jen! What happened wasn't something I wanted!"

"I didn't say it right. I mean, in a way you gave him a chance with her. That's what you really did at the fair. You kept your promise to him."

"And I was crazy to do it. She liked him the minute she met him."

"Then it can't be true love." Jen's cheeks stained red. "If it was me and you, you could introduce me to the most gorgeous movie star in the universe, and it wouldn't make any difference."

# 16

Today Tod came up to me and said, "Can we talk?" Then he just stood there, looking at me. We were in the corridor near the gym and people kept brushing into us. I waited. Finally he said, "I have something to say."

"Maybe not too pleasant?" I couldn't help thinking of the girl I'd seen him with. "I noticed you've been avoiding me," I said. I felt a swelling in my throat and behind my eyes. Until that moment I didn't know how miserable I'd been feeling. I said, "Look, Tod, why don't you just go to hell!" I started away, but he pulled me back, into a little alcove. Kids were all around us, pounding up and down the stairs.

Tod started telling me the whole story about Amos again—about how Amos saved his life, Amos this and Amos that, Amos his dearest best friend in the world and he owed Amos his life, and—

"I know all that," I said. "You told me."

"But not everything," he said. And then he stood there again and didn't speak.

"What?" I said.

And then he told me the only reason he met me was because of Amos. "Remember the day I came to the garage?"

85

he said. "I did that for Amos. And the first time I called
you—"

"For Amos?" I said.

"Yes. And then I talked to you in the cafeteria—that was
supposed to be for Amos, too."

It had all been a setup. Everything for Amos. He'd smiled
at me for Amos. Kissed me for Amos? I went almost deaf with
fury. He'd served me up to Amos as if I were a stupid hunk of
pot roast! "Where's your heart? Do you even have one?"
I shouted. I was so angry, so miserable, so humiliated. "What
about that girl? Where does she fit in? Did the two of you plan
this?"

He got this innocent, bewildered look on his face. "Girl?"

"Oh, don't lie to me on top of everything else! The girl I
see you with all the time."

"Jen?" he said. "You mean Jen? She's just a friend. What
about her?"

"Forget it!" At that point I was frantic. I'd said too much
and I was trying not to cry, trying to get out of this with a little
dignity and self-respect left. I said, "Look, leave me alone. Just
leave me alone!"

"Hilary," he said.

"I mean it," I said. And I walked away.

# 17

"Jen," Tod called. "She told me to go to hell."

"Hilary?" He nodded, and she put her arm through his. "I feel terrible! I gave you bad advice." She walked along with him. "I'm sure once she thinks it over, she'll realize how honest you were with her."

They walked to his house. "Can I come up with you? I'm curious about where you live. I'm curious about everything about you."

Upstairs, they peered into the empty refrigerator together. She sniffed the carton of milk. "Not much to choose from."

Tod made cracker and jelly sandwiches, and Jen popped them into her mouth as fast as he made them. "More! More!" She opened her mouth like a bird, trying to make him laugh.

And he did, he laughed, and then suddenly he put his head down on his arms and started crying.

Jen was there in a moment, her arms around him, her cheek next to his. "Please don't cry. I'm sure she's going to come back to you."

They went into his room. He turned on the stereo.

Jen sorted through his records. "Take anything you want," he said. "You can have anything there."

As suddenly as he'd started crying, he became manic. Talking, gesturing, giving away his records. Jen was a wonderful friend. He hadn't felt the least bit ashamed of crying in front of her. He paced up and down, talking, talking, talking, making plans—not about Hilary, no, he avoided that subject. He talked about college and travel and his relatives.

"I've got relatives all over this country. I've got family in England," he said. "One of these days I'm going to hop over there and look them all up."

He told Jen what a good friend she was and how much she'd done for him. "I have so much feeling about you." He was making a whole speech. The finale was that he hugged her. It was meant to be a friendly hug, a brotherly hug, but it turned into something else. They ended up really kissing.

That night he didn't sleep a lot. His dreams were full of women. Hilary . . . his mother . . . Jen . . . Loretta. Even Mrs. Pace got in there. In the morning he was groggy, staggering around, as if somebody had hit him in the head.

He fell asleep in history class. "If Mr. Ellerbee wouldn't mind . . ." Mr. Rosenberg was standing over him. "I hate to interrupt your nap, but we'd all appreciate the benefit of your wisdom. We've been talking about the Civil War, Mr. Ellerbee, and the question is—"

The question . . . Tod sat up and tried to concentrate. The question . . . what was the question? Was Jen the question? Was Hilary? What had he been thinking when he kissed Jen? Did he really feel that deeply about her? Then what about Hilary? Why *had* he kissed Jen?

Just for the pleasure of it? To make himself feel good? To mask his unhappiness? Some people drank to forget their unhappiness, some people ate. Was his way to fall into the arms of any willing female?

And then, right there in history class, he had a revelation: he had been acting just like his father. Tod Ellerbee as Bob Ellerbee. First the screwing up, then the depression and self-pity, then mania and turning to other women for comfort.

# 18

"Hilary's not here," Paula said, standing in the doorway. "Let's see, this is Tod, isn't it?"

Funny way of talking. *This is Tod?* As if she didn't know him or maybe didn't *want* to know him. Had Hilary said something to her?

"Hilary went up to the college for a concert with my father," Paula said.

"Your father's in a concert?"

"She went up to the college to *attend* a concert with my father. Beethoven piano sonatas."

Before she could ask him if he knew what a sonata was, he said, "Where on the campus would that be?"

"Lindsey Hall, the music building."

"Okay, thanks."

The auditorium in Lindsey Hall was like a church with high ceilings and round, stained-glass windows. On stage there were two grand pianos, one in the middle and one shoved off in a corner. Tod sat down in the back row. The seats next to him were empty. He looked around for Hilary, and saw Mrs. Pace. He walked over and talked to her.

"You haven't been to visit me for a while," she said.

They were talking about the hawk when a man wearing an open-necked shirt came out on the stage. Tod went back to his seat. The man wiped the piano keys with a rag. Tod thought he was the maintenance man until he sat down and the audience broke into applause. It was the pianist, Andrew Ragner.

Tod wasn't prepared for the sound. It was extraordinary. He'd never heard so much sound come out of a single instrument. Ragner was a show in himself. As he played, he threw his head up and over to one side, he pounced on the keys and brought his face down to the keyboard.

Next to Tod a ponytailed girl slid off her father's lap. On the floor she started playing with a Barbie doll, talking to herself. "And Barbie went for a ride in the spooky woods dum dum dum dum, and then Barbie met the horrible wolf with the sicko grin and she punched him out, pow!"

*And Hilary went for a ride in the spooky woods dum dum dum dum, and then Hilary met the horrible wolf Tod with the sicko grin and she punched him out, pow! pow! pow!*

The music went on and on, and after a while Tod stopped listening. He opened the program. *Allegro, Andante, Allegro molto e con brio. Finale—Prestissimo.* He felt a yawn coming and leaned his head down on his hand.

When he looked up, he saw Hilary sitting in the balcony, leaning over the railing. He saw her in profile, looking so proud, wearing her fan-shaped silver earrings.

At intermission he looked for her in the crowd coming down the stairs. He followed her down a corridor past a white plaster statue of the Winged Victory. "Hilary," he said.

She turned, dug her hands into her skirt pockets. Tod rolled and unrolled the program, feeling awkward and desperate. She looked past him. Was someone with her? Was Amos here? "Who'd you come with?" he said.

"What?" she said. "Who'd *you* come with?"

He tapped himself on the chest. "Me." Now it was her turn, but she didn't take it. He tried to read her face, to find a message in her eyes. Around them, people started back to the auditorium.

"When did you come?" she asked, giving him that rather cool, removed look. Did she mean, *Why are you bothering me?* "Did you know I was here?"

"Yes. That's why I came."

She started down the corridor and he went with her. "Where are you sitting? I'm upstairs."

"I know. I saw you."

An usher motioned them in. Hilary went up the stairs and Tod went back inside. A moment later he saw her taking her seat in the balcony. He saw her father sitting behind her.

The pianist came out and started playing. Tod watched Hilary. She was leaning on the railing again, her chin on her folded arms. Then, as the pianist's hands touched the keys, she looked down at Tod. They looked at each other. The music was all around them. And it was as if the music were talking for Tod, saying all the things he wanted to say to Hilary and could only say so clumsily.

During the second movement of the last sonata she left her seat. He became alarmed—was she leaving the concert? He stood up, but a moment later she dropped into the seat next to his. "Hello," she whispered.

# 19

The whole school knew about Tod and Hilary—not that they were broadcasting the news, but they were together all the time now. And when they weren't together, she wrote him notes.

"Hi, remember me? . . . The world and I are glad you're here." . . . Did you wear that sweater for me? (Because she had told him how good he looked in green.) . . . If we could see into the future, what would we see? Where will we be, Tod? She signed her notes "Your friend," or sometimes "Your best friend," or "Your best and loving friend."

"Why don't you ever write me a note?" she said. He tried, but everything he wrote came out stiff, like something a lawyer would write, and not at all the way he felt, which was happy. Well, almost happy.

The fly in the ointment was still the Amos factor. If only Amos had been in their school, he'd have known everything about Tod and Hilary. It would have been painful, but over with by now.

But Amos didn't know, and Tod didn't tell him. A dozen times Amos called Tod to talk about Hilary, and a dozen times Tod told himself, tell him! *Amos, nobody plans their feelings. What happened to us was something no one could have foreseen.*

But he didn't say it. Instead he hoped for a miracle. And when he went to Hilary's house, he deliberately walked by the grocery. Maybe at that very moment Amos would look out the window, see him, and lightning would strike: he'd understand everything. Or he'd come running out, calling, "Where're you going, my man?" And Tod would answer. *I'm going to see Hilary.*

*I didn't know you two were that kind of friends.*

*Yes, we are, Amos. We are that kind of friends.*

"Get me the spanner and the calipers, will you?" Hilary said.

"The what?" Tod asked. He was waiting for her to finish work.

She poked her head out from under a car, pointing to the red toolbox. "Second drawer from the left, ignoramus."

Carl looked up. "What are you doing, Hil? Are you working or fooling around?"

Tod took the hint and went outside to visit Tanya, who sprang up on the wire to greet him.

When Hilary was done working, they picked up a pizza and went to his house. His father was there in the kitchen, cooking. Tod set down the pizza.

"This is Hilary Goodman, Dad. Hilary, this is my father."

His father checked a pot. "Make yourself at home, Hilary. You and my son can set the table. And you can call me Bob."

*Great!* Tod thought. *He's turning on the charm.*

"We brought our own food."

"Pizza for supper?" his father said, giving Hilary a smile. "You kids need something more substantial than that." As if he cooked at all. As if he and Tod hadn't eaten countless pizzas at every meal and in every season of the year.

"Put the milk in a pitcher," his father said.

"What pitcher?"

"Put it into a glass, then." His father winked at Hilary.

Eating, his father was expansive. He told Hilary the old Richie Gribble story.

"They ended up in the same unit in Vietnam, Hilary," Tod said.

And then, predictably, his father said, "How's that for defying the law of averages?"

Later, over dessert, his father asked Hilary about her interests. "Are you a good student? You want to be a teacher?"

"An auto mechanic."

"Aw, come on!"

"She works in a garage, Dad," Tod said.

"No kidding." And then he said, "It's hard to believe a pretty girl like you would want to work in a grease-pit garage."

"Dad! That's baloney! You work in a factory. It's greasy, isn't it? There are plenty of women there—are they all ugly?"

His father looked at him then, and that look reminded Tod of where things stood between him and his father. The last time the two of them had concentrated on each other to the exclusion of everything else, they'd had their fists raised.

# 20

Tod introduced Jen to Hilary one day.

"So this is Hilary," Jen said. "I've heard a lot about you."

Hilary noticed Jen's sweater, a thick gray knit with tiny blue stars around the cuffs and the collar. "Is that handmade?"

"My grandmom made it."

"Oh. You're lucky. My grandmother's dead."

They walked down the hall together.

"I thought I'd hate you furiously," Jen said, "but I don't." She looked at Tod. "So everything's fixed up between you two?"

Tod was embarrassed. "Jen's been my Ann Landers," he said to Hilary.

"His Ann Landers plus!" Jen said. Was she thinking about the kiss?

"Listen, Jen, I want you to meet somebody," he said. "A terrific guy. His name is Amos." Hilary glanced at him doubtfully.

*But why shouldn't it work?* he thought. Jen and Amos were so perfectly matched. Both of them outgoing, both easy to be with, and both the same age. He imagined the four of them afterward, out together, remembering the way they'd met and laughing over it.

"This is someone you're going to like a lot," he said.

"Forget it," Jen said. "You might as well know, Hilary, for me it's either Tod or nobody."

Hilary looked a little taken aback, but after Jen left, Hilary said, "She's adorable."

When Tod finally got Jen and Amos together, it was a disaster. He came up to Amos's school holding Jen's hand. They waited near the steps while the school emptied out, the boys in dark trousers and dark jackets, the girls in pleated skirts and knee socks.

"Amos!" he called, and grabbed his friend's hand. Tod the matchmaker. "Meet Jen Kopp, Amos. Jen, this is Amos Vaccaro."

They both nodded stiffly. Tod had the feeling that if he let go of them, they'd fly off in opposite directions.

"Well, you guys, now I've got you together. You have a lot in common. Jen watches a lot of TV. So do you, Amos."

Amos unknotted his school tie. "No, I don't."

"What's your favorite show, Amos?" Tod plowed on. "Game shows? You like them, don't you, Jen? Everybody likes them."

"I never watch TV," Jen said.

The conversation, if you could call it that, just fell apart.

# 21

Yesterday Amos called. He had tickets for a concert. I could have said, Look, Amos, Tod and I are going together. I had that option, but I didn't say it. I didn't want to be the one to say it. I don't think it's right. Amos and Tod have been friends forever, and I don't think it's up to me to say it.

So I went to the concert with him. It was sold out, and we had to fight our way into the convention center. We were almost destroyed finding our seats, but it was all worth it when Bon Ami appeared. She floated down from the darkness above the stage in a shower of sparks and smoke, wearing tight, glittery green pants. She looked like a green snake. Then the Dwarfs pranced on, and the music came up fast and hot, rolled over me, pounded me, wave after wave after wave.

The music almost tore the roof off the building. I thought of the Ragner concert and how he wouldn't touch the keys until the last tiny rustle was stilled. And here we were, the whole audience, dancing on our seats.

When Bon Ami sang, "Love is my prayer to you," I almost cried. I thought of Tod first . . . then the boy I loved when I was twelve, who never knew I existed. And then I

98

*thought of my wonderful Nana, and I did start crying.* Love is my prayer to you, Nana. I'll never forget you.

*Amos wiped away my tears. We hugged. We danced and hugged, and we kissed. And it was wonderful! The music was all mixed in with the kiss. I was loose and sad and happy . . .*

*And now what?*

*It was the music . . . I tried to tell Amos. Did he believe me or did he think . . . ?*

*"It was the music, Amos . . . it was the music."* I kept saying it. *But the way Amos was looking at me, I don't think he understood.*

*And now I feel guilty. No, why should I feel guilty? . . . Confused, yes . . . but happy, too. The happy part is that it's so wonderful to love people and have people love you back. The other part is Tod. Can I really be in love with him if I can forget him that way?*

*But why can't I love him and Amos, too?*

*Why does love have to be stingy? Why can't it be like the music? Free and happy and there for everyone.*

# 22

"I went out with Amos last night," Hilary said. She and Tod were sitting on top of the falls. The wind was blowing, and she wrapped a scarf around her neck.

"You went out with Amos?" Tod said.

Looking away from him, she told him about the concert. "Amos had the tickets already. I just couldn't say no."

"What happened?" Tod said. He kept his voice level.

She pulled off the scarf. "What do you mean, what happened? We heard Bon Ami. . . . I can't believe you ever jumped off here."

He walked to the edge. Below him, the pool was almost dried up. "I don't believe it myself. . . . How come you go out with somebody else when you're going with me?"

"How come Amos doesn't know about us?"

He turned around. "I'm going to tell him."

He sat down next to her again. "What is it with you two?"

"We're friends," she said. "There's no reason why Amos and I can't be friends."

She was right. He knew she was right, only he had this nasty jealous streak. He picked up a stone and threw it over the edge, then listened until he heard the splash. "I'm glad you like Amos."

He thought of Jen, how she had liked Hilary. That was good. He wanted them all to be friends, only in the right combination. He rubbed his shoulder against Hilary's. "You know how I feel about Amos."

"He kissed me," Hilary said. "At the concert. And I kissed him back."

"Oh, hell," Tod said.

"Which means?"

"I don't know! I can't deal with this."


On Sunday, Loretta asked Tod to work extra hours. He went in at eleven and worked all day. It was busy busy, and he was glad. Whenever there was a break, he'd start thinking about Hilary . . . Hilary and Amos. What did it mean? It wasn't clear to him. She hadn't said, Oh, Tod, it was just an impulse of the moment. She hadn't said she wouldn't kiss Amos again. She hadn't said, Tod, it's you you you. She'd just given him the news, let it drop like acid rain.

After work, Loretta gave him a ride home. "How's Scott doing?" Tod asked, just to be saying something.

"My son? The usual." She gave a little laugh. "He left the phone off the hook the other night, and there I was trying to call home to talk to him. What if it had been an emergency? When I told him that, you know what he said?" She imitated Scott's drawly voice. "Soooo, Ma, I woulda diiied . . . Sometimes I think he acts more like three than fourteen. He's not really a bad kid. I know he's got a good heart"—she braked for a light—"but good Lord, sometimes he is thoughtless." As she parked in front of Tod's house, she said, "What's happening with Bob? I haven't heard from him in a while."

"My father? The same as usual."

"Yeah, just like Scott, his heart's in the right place." They both looked up at the windows. The lights were on.

"Come on up," Tod said. "Why do you let Bob jerk you around, Loretta? Why should he set the terms all the time? What is it, a one-way relationship?" Was he talking about his father and Loretta, or about himself and Hilary?

Upstairs he opened the door and called, "Where are you, Bob? You've got company."

"Loretta," his father said, coming out. He was wearing a bright red sweater and jeans.

"Where the hell have you been, Bob Ellerbee?" Loretta said. "Do I have to chase you all the time? My legs aren't as long as yours!" She punched him in the arm once, then twice, the second time a good hard punch. Then they walked into the kitchen arm-in-arm.

Tod went off to shower. "Good work, Ellerbee." Any day now he could hang out his sign: ADVICE FOR THE UNCERTAIN IN LOVE & MATTERS OF THE HEART. "Yeah," he said, "and you'll be your own first client."

Tod and Hilary walked across the campus to her father's office. Hilary was taking her father to a doctor's appointment. "What time?" Tod asked.

She glanced at her watch. "Oh, I'm early."

The campus was like a park in the middle of the city. "These old buildings are great, aren't they?" Hilary said.

"Yeah, I really like them. I like the ivy." Polite conversation. There was a strain between them. Those few words: *He kissed me . . . I kissed him back.* They hadn't mentioned it again—what was there to say? What could he say that wouldn't sound stupid or possessive or bullying? I forbid you to kiss Amos! Or anybody else! Did anybody say things like that anymore? She had a right to kiss whoever she wanted to. He didn't have to like it—he didn't like it. Period. And that's where they stood now—right on that period.

Her father's office was in Mere Bailly Hall. Tod glanced into a classroom as he and Hilary passed. The professor standing in front, the students sprawled in their seats. He tried to imagine himself here, in college, and he couldn't make it seem real. Was he really going to college? Was he really going to be a lawyer?

Professor Goodman's office was in the basement, a stuffy little room crowded with a desk and filing cabinets. Tod studied the bulletin board behind the door. "Who's this Finley character coming to speak?"

"A famous economist. One of my father's idols. Right up there with Galbraith." She sat down in her father's chair and put her feet up on the desk. "So what can I do for you, young man?"

She was giving him a quiet, sweet look, and suddenly he loved her so much he became convinced that she was going to tell him something awful. "So, Hilary," he said, sounding harsher than he meant to, "let's have it. Where do we stand?"

"I'm sitting. You're standing. Ooops, sorry. Feeble joke. I should leave the jokes to Amos."

There it was. Amos's name dropped between them like a brick off a wall.

Hilary stood up and opened a window. A breeze blew in, stirring papers on the desk. "Maybe you don't realize it, Tod, but I never had a boyfriend before you." She was talking with her back to him. "They zapped me at my other school, they had me down for a dyke because I like motors and stuff. Then I met you and it was really, really nice."

"Was?" he said, and he had to sit down he got so scared.

"And then you brought Amos into it, and you made us a threesome."

"Wait a minute. I explained that to you. Are you forgetting how this whole thing started?"

"I didn't forget anything. I'm just trying to tell you something about the concert, about the kiss." She sat near him on the edge of the desk. "What I think is—maybe I got greedy. Maybe I was making up for lost time, you know . . . never having a boyfriend." She balanced a ruler on one finger. "All of a sudden, I had you and I had Amos and I thought, *Why not? I'm in hog heaven.*"

He should have laughed. Instead he said, "I'm not sharing."

And she blew up. "Let me finish!" She pointed the ruler at him. "This isn't easy for me, Tod. I finally decided . . . I can't do that."

"Can't do what?"

"Can't have you both."

"And so—?"

"And so—" she said. "You."

"Me?"

"Yeah, you." She jabbed him with the ruler. "What do you think?"

"I think I think too much," he said, and then he kissed her.

Later, as they waited for her father at the doctor's, Hilary showed Tod a gold locket. It was a double-heart locket on a gold chain. "Turn it over," she said.

He read the inscription on the back: TO H.G. WITH LOVE FOREVER FROM A.V. "Amos?" he said.

She nodded. "Open it." Inside there was a picture of Amos and space for another. "I told him I couldn't take a present like this. I tried to give it back to him. I said he had to return it."

"What did he say?"

"What didn't he say? He said he bought it for me. He said it was mine, and he would never take it back. Never! You should have heard him. You know Amos. He was incredibly insistent. He said he'd sooner throw it away. He said there was no one else he'd give this to. No one else he'd ever thought of giving something like this." Hilary looked upset. "In a way, I suppose I brought it on myself . . . I never dreamed he'd go out and do this! And so tell me, Tod, now what do I do?"

# 23

On the way home from school Tod detoured to Bishop Hayes High. He went into the office and asked for Amos. Behind the long desk a portrait of Pope John Paul, wearing white and blessing the faithful in Mexico, hung on the wall. The secretary checked a schedule and told him Amos was at a drama club meeting.

In the auditorium a scattering of kids sat in the first few rows. As Tod came in, Amos was just taking the stage. He pulled a stool around and sat down, slumped down. His face changed, went slack, his mouth fell open. Tod got scared. He thought something had happened. Then a girl with a big purple ribbon in her hair called out, "That's great, Amos."

Amos looked up and shook his fist. "Shadd up," he sputtered in a shaking voice. "Shadd up!" His head shook, and he did something to his face that make him look toothless and trembly. "Old Rendo warns you young ones," Amos said in a quivering but demanding voice, "you sappy, snot-nosed kids. Old Rendo knows about you. Old Rendo is five hundred and five years old. That's a lot of experience. That's a lot of streets crossed.

That's a lot of cheeseburgers." He stood, holding on to the stool.

It was funny, but there was also something a little scary and real about it.

"Time is passing. Old Rendo says, don't say no! Say yes! Yes to fun! Yes to love! Yes to life!" Someone cheered. Someone else hissed. *"Tempus fugit,"* Amos cried, raising his hand. "Time flies. *Tempus fugit, fugit,* it fugits furiously!"

When Amos came off the stage, a husky boy and the girl with the purple ribbon ran up and hugged him. "How'd I do? How'd I do?" Amos said. And then he saw Tod, and it was as if his face stopped.

"Hi," Tod said. "You busy?" Amos just looked at him. His silence made Tod uncomfortable. What was he thinking? Tod put an arm across Amos's shoulder. He wanted to vault across the empty space he suddenly felt between them. "You were terrific. I can't believe the way you did that old man."

"Katie," Amos said to the girl with the purple ribbon. "Meet Tod, a friend of mine."

"You're friends with this guy?" Katie said to Tod. She gave Amos an elbow. "I feel sorry for you."

"Man, I'm beat," Amos said to her. "Maybe Old Rendo is taking me over. I feel about five hundred years old today."

"You look it," Katie said. "Haw haw haw."

After the rehearsal Tod and Amos left together. They stopped in a diner and took a booth. Amos wolfed down a couple of hamburgers and fries. Tod pushed around his food. *I saw Hilary the other day, Amos, and . . .*

*Amos, I don't want to hurt you, but I'm going to put my cards on the table . . .*

*Look, old man, we've been friends for a long time and there's no good way to say this . . .*

"I went out to the falls a few days ago," Tod said to break the silence. He didn't say anything about Hilary's being there with him. "You should see it, hardly any water now."

"What'd you go there for?"

"I don't know. Maybe to think about that day when you saved my life."

Amos was silent. Then he said, "That was something, wasn't it?"

"It sure was," Tod agreed.

Amos wiped his mouth. "I made a fool of myself with Hilary," he said abruptly. "I gave her a locket with my picture in it. She didn't want to take it, but I made her keep it."

"Amos," Tod began, "I want to tell you something—"

"Wait," Amos said. "Wait." He reached into his pocket. "I want you to do something for me." He brought out a fan-shaped silver earring. Tod recognized it.

"It's Hilary's," Amos said. "I want you to give it back to her."

"Me?" Tod rolled the can of soda between his palms.

"She dropped it," Amos said. "Did she tell you we went to the Bon Ami concert? I was going to give it back to her but . . . but . . . you do it," he said abruptly.

And then he was Old Rendo again. "You crazy kids! Always losing things. Never see what's in front of your nose. Give the earring back to the pretty girl!" He cackled and slid it across the table, his hand shaking. "You tell her she's ten stars, boy, tell her Old Rendo said it. You going to tell her that, boy? You listening, boy?"

"Listening," Tod said. A laugh caught in his throat.

Amos—or was it Old Rendo?—crumpled his napkin. And in that moment Tod saw in Amos's face that he understood everything, understood about himself and Hilary, and about Hilary and Tod—and even why Tod hadn't told him everything. It was all there on Amos's face, in his eyes. Not even Old Rendo could hide the truth.

# 24

"What's the matter, old man?" his father asked. "Why the long face?" They were eating in Margo's, a diner that his father was fond of.

Tod studied the menu. Maybe he should call Amos. *You know how I feel about you, Amos, and that's why I'm telling you you're going to get over this thing with Hilary. You're going to find another girl. And you're going to be crazy about her and you're going to look back and be glad because that girl is going to love you back.* "What're you having, Dad?"

"Probably the beef stew."

The food came. They ate without too much conversation. When he was done, Tod's father asked for coffee. "You want some pie, Tod?" Margo asked. "It's apple raisin today."

"Give it to him with vanilla ice cream," his father said. "No dessert for me." He lit a cigarette.

"You shouldn't smoke so much," she said.

His father took a deep puff and winked at her.

"She's right," Tod said. "Why don't you quit?"

His father picked a bit of tobacco from his lip. "I'll tell you something. If you really cared, I'd stop."

110

Tod pushed his pie away. This was too much. He felt accused by everyone. First Amos, with his sad eyes. Now his father. "I can't believe I'm hearing this, Dad. You're blaming your habit on me? What makes you think I don't care?"

His father took another deep puff. "Hey, I've got a memory." He held up his fist. "Remember?"

"I'm sorry about that," Tod said stiffly.

"I don't want apologies. It's not the insolence I mind— that's typical teenage crap. What I mind is what's underneath."

"And what's that?"

His father sat back. "Oh, I don't know," he said in a weary voice. "Just the thought that you don't give a damn about me."

What was his father doing, *begging*? And what was he supposed to say? *I care. I care. I care!* How many times would he have to say it? It felt like blackmail. It made him mad and he clammed up.

Tod put a stack of empty shoeboxes away on a low shelf. The regular Friday night men's league had taken four lanes, and the thud and boom of bowling balls filled the air.

Hilary leaned back against the counter. "How're you doing?" she called to Scott, who was playing a computer game nearby.

"I just won a free game," Scott said. "You want to play?"

"Thanks, I'll pass," Hilary said.

"It's a good game, almost as good as bowling. Good for coordination, concentration, cooperation. Anybody can play it," Scott said coaxingly.

Tod glanced over. Was that a genuine smile on Scott's blubbery lips?

"You don't need a uniform, Hilary," Scott went on. "You don't need a coach, you don't even need a team. You can have fun immediately."

"I bet you're good."

"Yeah," Scott said, trying unsuccessfully to look modest. "I am." And then, acknowledging Tod for the first time, he said, "You should get your boyfriend to play with you."

"Scott doesn't seem like such a bad person," Hilary said later. "I expected him to be a real creep from the things you've told me."

"He acted civilized today. That was a five-minute special for you."

"Oh, come on," she scoffed. As they stood talking by the car, she braided her hair and tucked it under her cap. She was on her way to work. "Maybe you've been unfair to him." They kissed, and she glanced at her watch. "Two more minutes . . ."

He didn't want to let her go. The moment she got behind the wheel, she would forget him. He had seen her that way—not listening to the conversation, shaking her hair impatiently out of her face, focused completely on driving.

"You didn't say anything at all about us to Amos?" she said. They'd talked about it earlier.

"I didn't have to. If you'd been there and seen his face when he gave me your earring, Hil—" He stopped. Was it fair to talk about Amos's pain to her?

"I suppose I should put that locket in a drawer somewhere and forget it for now," Hilary said.

"Yeah, wait until—just wait a while, anyway." He

meant until Amos could take the hurt of having the locket returned to him. But then he imagined it in a drawer, and he thought that every time Hilary opened the drawer she'd see those linked hearts and think of Amos. And it alarmed him. There was that spark of jealousy in him, always waiting to be ignited.

Was that why he didn't get around to calling Amos until the middle of the week? He knew what he wanted to say. *Listen, Amos, I know this is hard to hear, and I'm not the guy you want to hear reassurance from right now, but I love you and—*

Would he say that? Say he loved Amos? When he wouldn't say it to his own father? He meant it, he felt it, but he'd never said it to anyone. Not even Hilary.

When he finally called Amos, it was Amy who answered the phone. "Tod, Amos isn't here."

"Well, tell him to call me when he gets in."

"He's in the hospital, Tod. He's in St. Francis. He was admitted last night. Mom and Dad took him to the emergency room around seven o'clock."

The first thing Tod thought was terrifying—Amos had tried to kill himself. He saw Amos lying on the bathroom floor, his wrists bleeding, "saw" it so vividly he could almost feel the coolness of the tiles. And he remembered what Amos had said to him once about Hilary. *You don't know how I feel, man. I'd give my life for her. . . .*

"Last night at supper," Amy said. "Amos suddenly couldn't breathe. At first we thought he'd swallowed something and he was choking on it. Mom and Dad did the Heimlich maneuver on him. But it didn't help. He still couldn't breathe. Then we thought he was having an asthma attack, and it was so bad Mom and Dad decided

to get him over to the emergency room. They're still at
the hospital with him.''

"Well, what is it?'' Tod asked. He couldn't grasp the
idea that Amos was in the hospital. "Was it an asthma
attack?''

"No. Don't know what it is, Tod. You know Amos is
allergic to a million things. He just stopped having shots
a couple years ago. The doctor said maybe he's having a
reaction to something in the environment or something
he ate. They're running a bunch of tests on him today.
Tomorrow we'll know something. And by Thursday, I
guarantee you, he'll be home. You know Amos. He's not
going to miss Thanksgiving.''

"This is the one holiday I like,'' Tod's father said,
looking around the table. Loretta, Scott, Tod, and Bob
were downtown at White's Inn, where they served an
old-fashioned Thanksgiving dinner with giblet stuffing,
candied sweet potatoes, homemade cranberry sauce, and
three kinds of pie.

"Christmas is greed,'' Bob went on. "New Year's
reminds you that you're getting older, Independence Day
is false sentiment, and Veterans Day—pure hypocrisy.
Now, Thanksgiving is different. All over the country we
Americans do what we're expected to do—we pig out.
Here's to pumpkin, mince, and lemon meringue,'' Bob
raised his glass in a toast. Then they all clinked their
glasses.

"And a happy Thanksgiving to all of us,'' Tod said.

So far, things had gone well. Nobody had gotten
mad at anybody. It usually wasn't that congenial when
the four of them got together. Too many underground
currents.

"I want to tell you all something," Loretta said. "I'm thinking about opening an office cleaning business. It'll be risky, I'll have to borrow money, but I've been looking into it, and there's a market—"

"What do you want to do that for?" Scott said. "You mean you'd quit your job? You're always saying we don't have any money." His pouty lips trembled indignantly.

"If things work out, Scottie, there'd be a place for you in the business. Which would be good for both of us. And then, maybe we'll have a little more security than we do now. . . . What do you think, Bob?"

"More power to you, Loretta. If anybody has the energy to carry it off, you do."

His father was in a good mood, Tod thought, which was probably a big reason why the four of them managed to get through the meal without a single real flare-up.

After dessert Tod went out to watch the parade down Gore Avenue, which had been closed off to traffic. A huge inflated turkey bobbed over the rooftops. People were lined up on both sides of the street, watching the marchers. The Legion Band marched by. Flags . . . uniforms . . . baton twirlers . . . Tod walked along the edge of the crowd. He saw Jen perched on a light pole.

He tugged at her foot and she looked down. "Hi," he said. "I haven't seen you in a while." A group of people dressed as Pilgrims and Indians went past. Behind them was a troop of Girl Scouts. "Where've you been hiding?" Tod said. "Have you forgotten me and the Tod Ellerbee Fan Club?"

"Disbanded!" A flush came up on Jen's smooth cheeks. She dropped down. He put his arm around her and tried to give her a kiss, but she pulled away and stuck out her hand for him to shake.

"What's this?" he said. "Why the formality? Are you mad or something?"

"Not mad. Just realistic."

He pulled her braids playfully.

"Stop that! Don't treat me like a baby."

"Sorry." He pulled back his hands.

"I finally figured out our problem, Tod. I've been up front with you, but you want to deny that you're attracted to me."

"Who's denying it? I like you. I'm not trying to deny it."

"Oh, sure, when it suits you, and when it doesn't suit you, you forget me. Right? I thought we were friends. But what kind of friends are we if you never call me? When was the last time you came looking for me? When was the last time you even thought about me? I know about Hilary, but that's not the point. You want it all to come from me. Do you want to laugh? Go ahead, Tod! I know what you think. Cute little Jen."

"No," he protested, but he had been thinking just that.

"I cried over you, Tod, but I'm not crying anymore. I'm over you. But we can still be friends. Only it's not going to be one way anymore. You've got to do something, too." She looked past him. "Who's that guy staring at us? Someone you know?"

It was Scott, ambling toward them. "I thought you were going with Bob and Loretta," Tod said.

"It's a free country." Scott smiled at Jen.

The Vietnam veterans contingent was passing. "Oh, there's my father," Jen said. She waved. "Daddy!" A tall man pushing another veteran in a wheelchair looked up and waved back.

"How come Bob doesn't march?" Scott said to Tod.

Tod shrugged. "Why don't you ask him?"

Scott moved around toward Jen. "What branch of the service was your father in?"

"He was on a helicopter crew."

"No kidding! I want to go in the air force, myself."

That was news to Tod.

"How old was your father when he joined up?" Scott said to Jen.

"I'm not sure. Come on, I'll ask him." The two of them moved along, following the marchers. Jen turned. "Tod? Don't forget what I said."

# 25

At the end of the week Amos was still in the hospital, and Tod went to see him. He was on the fourth floor, pediatric ward. There were four beds in the room, only two of them occupied. A boy with a cast on his leg sat in a chair by the window. "Is Amos Vaccaro in this room?" Tod said.

The boy looked up. "They took him for tests a while ago. He ought to be back pretty soon."

Tod waited in the hall near the elevators. *Ding!* The doors opened and people poured out. A nurse pushed a wheelchair with an old woman in a white hospital gown down the hall. The old woman was tiny and hunched over, like a dried-out yellow insect. Tod looked away. It was uncomfortably hot. He took off his jacket and pushed up his sweater sleeves. *Ding!* The elevator doors opened again, and there was Amos being wheeled out by a candy striper.

Tod wasn't prepared for the shock of seeing Amos in a wheelchair. He strode forward. "Amos!"

Amos pulled Tod down and hugged him. All the constraint from their last meeting was gone.

"This is my man Tod," he said to the girl pushing him. His voice had a hoarse, gaspy quality. "This is Brenda, Tod." She was a lanky girl with a lot of color in her face. Next to her, Amos looked sallow. "She's in love with me, aren't you, Brenda?"

"I told you, I have a boyfriend," Brenda said primly. She wore a necklace of colored beads over her pink and white uniform.

As she wheeled Amos to his room, Tod walked alongside, a hand on Amos's shoulder.

"I'm going to be out of here in a couple days, Tod," Amos said. He stopped to catch his breath. "As soon as they get these tests over with, I'm—"

"You're not supposed to talk so much," Brenda interrupted.

"But I like to talk," Amos said. "Tell her how much I like to talk, Tod."

"Oh, he likes to talk, all right," Tod said.

"I know. I could tell," Brenda said.

In his room Amos got into bed. "Bye, Brenda, will I see you again?"

"Probably not," she said, standing in the doorway. "I'm going onto another ward next time I come in."

"Break my heart, go ahead."

"Oh, now, Amos," she said, "don't talk like that."

He kept up the flirtation until Brenda left. Then he lay back against the pillows with a sigh. "Man . . . they tire you out in this place. Sit down, sit down, where you going?"

Tod pulled a chair up next to the bed. "So what's going on?"

"Who knows? They've been taking pictures and sticking needles in me right and left. Needle park, that's me.

They woke me up this morning, they had a needle for me before breakfast." Amos looked indignant. "When I get out of here, I'll have a million ideas for running a better hospital, Tod."

"Amy told me what happened," Tod said.

"Man, it was so weird. I wasn't sick! I was just sitting there, talking . . . and then I was under the table. Just like that, like somebody smacked me with a board. I was gone." He stopped and caught his breath again. "All the air went out of me. I never had anything like that before." He gestured toward his throat. "I couldn't breathe. Man, it was scary."

When Tod left, Amos wanted to walk to the elevator with him, but a gray-haired nurse came running after him. "No, no, no, no," she called. "Wheelchair for you, young man. Doctor's orders!"

"Aw, come on, Sally, I just want to see my buddy to the elevator."

"Fine. Stand right there until I get the wheelchair."

"Hard as nails, aren't you?" Amos said. "I can't take a sip of water without your permission."

"That's right," Sally said, bringing over a wheelchair. "I'm the boss."

He held up his wrist with the plastic ID bracelet. "See my handcuffs?" But he didn't protest when Sally helped him into the wheelchair.

# 26

Amos has been in the hospital for a week, and I still haven't gone to see him. I'm ashamed of myself. I should go, but I can't. It's Nana. It's been a year since she died, and I still dread even going past the hospital.

That day, the day Nana died, I was in the hospital down the hall, and I heard someone yelling, "Code Blue! Code Blue!" Suddenly all these people in white uniforms, doctors and nurses and aides, rushed by me and into Nana's room. I ran after them. I saw them all around her bed, all these large people beating on her. Pounding on her chest. Her foot was sticking out of the covers at the bottom of the bed, her tiny bony foot bouncing up and down. I remember thinking, Poor foot. And then, then just as suddenly as it started, it all stopped. They drew the curtain and they left.

And I went forward, toward Nana. I walked slowly, so slowly. I wasn't feeling anything. I pushed the curtain aside. I saw her lying in the bed. Her mouth was open. Her long gray hair was spread out.

Then a doctor came in and told me to go out. I went into the hall and someone else said, "You're the granddaughter, aren't you? I'm sorry."

And then the feeling came. I knew she was dead. And ever since I can't even go near a hospital.

121

# 27

Tod met Amy on the elevator. He hugged her. "Did you just come?"

She shook her head. "No, Mom and I have been here for a while. I was in the cafeteria."

Amos's family were rotating their visits to make sure that he had company as much as possible. Tod kept running into aunts and uncles and cousins of Amos's.

Amy was all in cheerful yellows and reds, but her face looked bad, somehow swollen.

"I didn't sleep too much last night. I kept waking up and thinking about my brother. He's had so many tests and they haven't found out anything. I believe in science. There's an answer for everything, isn't there? Only *this*, this whatever-it-is—why can't they tell us what's wrong with him? He's just so tired all the time. You know they thought it might be mononucleosis for a while."

"I know," Tod said. "He had those bone marrow tests."

"They were terrible," Amy said. "I mean, they're painful. But at least if it had been that . . . how can they cure him if they don't even have a name for what he's got?"

In Amos's room his mother kissed Tod and patted his shoulder. "I'm going, I'm going. Amy, get your coat, Tod's here now." She fixed Amos's covers. "I know you boys have things to talk about."

Tod walked to the door with her.

"It's good that you come to see him," she said. "His other friends come now and then, but you come all the time. You don't know how much he looks forward to it."

When Tod went back in, Amos was out of bed. "Is Ma gone? Come on, we'll take a walk." His voice was peculiar. When Tod tried to describe it to Hilary later, he said it was like a robot's voice, but that sounded inhuman. It was Amos's voice, but without any bounce to it, without any vibration or inflection.

Amos pulled the IV trolley. "Come on, Bozo."

"Shouldn't you be in the wheelchair?" Tod said.

"Shut up. They got big ears around here . . . Big Sister is watching all the time." And it was true. When they came around the corner, gray-haired Sally and another nurse were waiting for him. "Into bed with you," Sally said. She held his elbow. "Why do you give us so much trouble?"

"Tell me what's wrong with me . . . and I promise I'll be good. Cure me . . . or let me go." Everything he said was filled with pauses for breath.

In his room Amos fell back against the pillows and closed his eyes.

"Hilary says hello," Tod said. Amos's eyes flicked open. "I saw her today. She said to be sure to say hi."

"She's still mad at me, isn't she?"

"She didn't say that. She told me to be sure to say hello to Amos." It was an odd situation, Tod thought. A little sticky. Amos knew about him and Hilary, but yet because he was sick, Tod was reluctant to say too much. He didn't want to sound too happy. That would just be rubbing salt in the wound. "If I see her, you want me to say anything to her for you? You want to send her a message or something?"

Amos nodded and pushed himself up on his elbows. "Tell her . . . tell her I still admire her more than any other girl I know."

# 28

The first thing Tod saw when he walked into the room was a big green oxygen tank behind the bed. "So what's this?" Tod said, looking at the dials and hoses.

"That green thing?" Amos wheezed. He had an oxygen mask in his hand. "That's King Kong. A friend for Bozo, the IV."

"It's a regular zoo in here," Tod said, but he was scared.

Amos put on the oxygen mask. "I've been thinking about food," he said from behind it. "Real food. Pizza with pepperoni and sausage . . . fries . . . Polish pickles." Behind the mask, his voice was muffled. "What'd you have for lunch today, Tod?"

"You don't want to know, Amos."

"On Tuesdays, my school . . . macaroni and cheese. Better than Ma's. Don't tell . . . her."

"You like school lunches?" It was a relief to have something he could tease Amos about. "Now that's what I call sick." *Sick.* It was nearly the only time he referred to Amos's sickness, his illness, his whatever-it-was-ness. Nobody had put a name to it yet.

125

\*     \*     \*

"Look who came to see me," Amos said. He'd been moved into a private room. For a moment Tod didn't see Hilary, because a couple of meaty-looking guys from Amos's school were also visiting, a couple of football players.

Hilary was perched on the windowsill. "The bad penny," she said, raising her hand in greeting to Tod. His response was equally casual. She hadn't told him she was going to come, but it was as if the moment Tod had appeared, they had silently agreed not to act like a couple.

Amos introduced everybody. "Visiting me is a penance for Kevin and Jimmy's sins," he told Tod and Hilary. He put on the oxygen mask. "Tell my friends . . . about your sins. I bet Father Dan groans when he sees . . . you guys coming to confession."

When his school friends left, Tod handed Amos a couple of TV magazines. Whenever he visited, Tod brought Amos some little thing. It had been his father's suggestion. It made Tod remember how, years ago, he used to look forward to the gifts his father brought him when he was sick.

"Sit down . . . take a load off," Amos said. There was color in his face. It was because of Hilary, Tod thought. But he talked as if every word cost him an effort. "Look at . . . that guy," he said to Hilary. "He won't sit . . . down."

Tod went out in the hall to get a drink of water. Should he stay? Being there with Hilary bothered him, or rather he was afraid it bothered Amos. Not that Amos seemed upset, but then he was an actor, wasn't he? Tod and Hilary were putting on a pretty good act themselves. They didn't talk. They didn't look at each other.

She left before Tod. "Well, now that I've broken the ice, I'll be back. Or no, I have a better idea. You be home next time I see you. Okay?"

Amos reached out his hand. "Happy . . . glad you came, Hilary, very happy."

"I'm glad, too," she said. And she went, passing Tod without a word.

Tod sat down, feeling a little limp. He hadn't realized how tense he'd been with Hilary there. "So what'd they do to you today? More tests, or what?"

Amos waved his hand dismissively and closed his eyes. Shutting Tod out. "I don't want to talk about the hospital . . . now, man." He turned on his side, away from Tod.

Hilary was waiting for Tod downstairs. "Come on," she said, "let's get out of here." She pushed through the doors. Outside, she ran. At the car she stopped and drew in breath after breath of air.

"Were you surprised to see me?" she said. "I had to come. I woke up this morning and I heard Nana saying, 'Hilary, shame on you.' "

"A dream," Tod said.

"I don't know. I thought I was awake." She took Tod's arm. "He looks so sick. You didn't tell me how awful he looks."

"He looked better today," Tod said.

"Better? I don't believe it."

"He looked *much* better today."

"Really?"

"Yes. Because you were there."

"Well, he had other visitors. Those two guys . . ."

"No," Tod said. "It was because of you."

# 29

Tod and I don't visit Amos together. If he's there when I come in, he leaves. I do the same if it's the other way around. We've never talked about it, we didn't make an agreement or anything, but it's what we do. And in front of Amos we have this little act going. "Hi . . . oh, hi . . ." As if we never see each other. As if we're no more than casual friends. As if the only time we run into one another is right there, in Amos's room.

Are we lying to him? It's at least a white lie, but I think it's the right thing to do. What's the alternative—flaunt ourselves in front of Amos's face? That would be cruel.

I notice that Amos goes right along with our act. Or at least he doesn't talk about Tod and me in the same breath anymore.

The other day he said to me, "You like me a little, don't you?" It was supposed to come out as a joke—he wriggled his eyebrows like Groucho Marx.

I said, "I don't like you a little, Amos. I like you a lot."

What a reward I got for saying the truth! His whole face lit up, as if I'd given him something that was beyond belief. It's so easy to make him happy. Why did I have to be prompted to say it? Why couldn't I have just said it spontaneously? I have to remember to do that more often, say the things I'm really feeling to Amos. It's little enough if it can make him so happy.

128

# 30

Tod and Hilary fell into the habit of comparing notes about Amos. "Did you think he looked any better, Tod?"

"I didn't, but when you see someone almost every day, it's hard to tell."

Hilary nodded. "I know. What I do is try to remember something specific to compare about him from one day to the next, like how many words he gets out before he sticks that mask on his face. Then I can tell if he's any stronger."

"Is he?"

She shook her head. "I don't think so."

"What does he talk about to you?"

"Oh, all kinds of things. Food is a big one. He thinks food is going to cure him."

"Did I tell you I brought him french fries?" Tod said.

"Did he eat them?"

"One or two."

"He dreams about food a lot. We got into this thing of telling each other our dreams. I tell him a dream I had, and then he tells me one he had."

"What kind of dreams?" That jealous spark in his heart flared up. She had never told him any of her dreams.

"Oh, you know how crazy dreams are. Last night I dreamed someone called me on the phone and said something about having my cars ready. 'What cars?' I said. 'The Mercedes,' he said. And I said, 'You must have the wrong person.' " Hilary laughed. "Then I woke up and I thought, Why'd I say that? I could have had a Mercedes!"

A few afternoons later they met in the hospital lobby by chance. "Going up or coming down?" Tod asked.

"Up," Hilary said.

"Me, too."

"Oh . . ." She looked at him questioningly. "What do you think?"

"Let's both go up. It would be phony not to." He set her cap straight on her head and they hugged. "I'll just stay for a few minutes."

The fourth-floor corridor was crowded with gurneys and empty hospital beds. Amos was in a wheelchair next to his bed. The oxygen mask was in his lap. "Both of you," he said. Was he pleased? It was hard to tell.

"Hello, old man." Tod put a bag with cream cakes on the bedside table.

Hilary sat down next to Amos and began talking. "Well, did you watch our favorite show last night? Wasn't that wild?"

"I liked it . . . the older women . . . and Alex . . ."

Tod stopped pacing. He had half-watched the show while he was doing homework. A flashback story of seventeen-year-old Alex in love with a woman twenty years older. A little farfetched, but not entirely, Tod had thought, thinking of Loretta and himself. Amos hadn't entered his mind until now.

"A lot of truth," Amos said. It was painful to hear his breathing.

Tod sat down on the floor with his back against the closet. There was nothing for him to do. Hilary was doing it all. She amazed Tod. He always had to struggle to keep the conversation going, but Hilary just zoomed along, as if she were at the wheel of a car. She went from three funny items she'd pulled out of the newspaper, to a weird situation Paula had once gotten into with a guy who borrowed her car for a day, to a book she was reading and hating ("That's why I keep reading it. It's so much fun to hate something so thoroughly."), to the Multimedia Club production.

"They're calling for a volunteer to play a rooster in their new production. Amos, what do you think? You want to coach me?"

In the old days Amos would have flapped his wings and crowed at the top of his lungs. Now he contented himself with a nod and a tiny chuckle. Everything he did had become economical, minimal. When he gestured, he raised a finger instead of a hand. When he spoke, it was with the fewest words. And Tod noticed that he never finished anything he ate—it was a bite of cream cake, a spoonful of Jell-O, a sip of juice.

Toward the end of that week the doctors told the family that Amos's heart was enlarged, and a heart-monitoring machine was moved into the room. The doctors suspected that Amos had had rheumatic fever when he was small. "And we didn't know it," Amy said to Tod. "He was always skinny and had a lot more colds than I did," she added.

An enlarged heart sounded alarming to Tod, but oddly enough the news cheered Amos. "Got something . . . to look for now. Once they figure out . . . why . . . got it beat, man."

Optimism gave Amos an appetite or at least the idea of an appetite. When the aide came around with the menu for the next day, he sat there and marked everything on the sheet. *Good!* Tod thought. Because, although Amos talked about food and there was always food by his bed brought in by his family—fresh fruit, and soup in thermoses, and little cakes—he had lost weight. A lot of weight. He had never been fat—if anything, skinny. But now he had gone beyond skinny or even scrawny. His arms were sticklike, his cheekbones stuck out, his eyes looked enormous in his face. Tod had the queasy feeling that every time he saw Amos, he had shrunk a little more.

# 31

Tod walked into Amos's room just as Hilary was leaving. Actually he walked in on her kissing Amos. Tod didn't say anything. What was there to say? She was kissing Amos good-bye. Only, the way she bent over him and put her hands around his face and let her lips linger on his—was that necessary?

Tod reproached himself for being stingy. How much of Hilary did Amos have? A few minutes a day? A few hours a week? Whereas he, Tod, was with her all the time. In school, between classes they rushed to their special meeting place, the big window on the second floor that overlooked the playing field. They saw each other weekends, and when they weren't together in the evenings, they talked on the phone.

That evening when Hilary called, he was going to say something about the kiss, actually something to show that it hadn't bothered him, something light and offhand. *How is it, kissing Amos? . . . Is he a six? An eight?* Before he could say anything, though, Hilary started analyzing her visit to Amos. "He was awfully tired today, did you notice? I think I cheered him up. I'd hate to think I was

133

tiring him out more. I want to take his mind off being sick. That's the point, isn't it?"

"Yeah, sure."

She couldn't stop picking her visit apart. She thought he'd looked a little paler than the last time. Did Tod agree? Had he noticed that Amos used the oxygen mask more? Was he getting weaker? Had Tod talked to anyone in the family lately about what was going on? "I pray for him every night," she said.

Tod never prayed. Maybe when he was very small he had, but since he started thinking for himself, he just couldn't believe in Someone up there, directing all the screwed-up traffic down here.

Almost all he and Hilary seemed to talk about lately was Amos. One day, right in the middle of a kiss, she had drawn back and said, "I just find it unbelievable that he is still in the hospital." So what was Tod supposed to think? Was she kissing him or mulling over Amos?

"I heard there's a new doctor on his case," she said now, "a specialist. Maybe they'll finally figure out what's wrong with him."

Tod listened another few moments in silence, then burst out, "Is it okay if we don't talk about Amos? I mean, for five lousy minutes can we not talk about the guy?"

There was a sudden quiet on the other end of the phone.

"Hello?" he said.

"Why're you mad?"

"All I said was, let's not talk about Amos for five minutes. That doesn't seem unreasonable."

"Okay. Right. Start counting. What do you want to talk about?"

"Anything."

"Well, you pick the subject. You're the one who wanted to—"

"Oh, come on, what is this? Now we can't talk unless it's something *I* want to talk about? Get off it!"

"I knew you were mad!"

"I told you I'm not mad. I just said—"

"I know what you said, and you are, too, mad."

"Hilary, you're driving me wacko!"

"Tod, you're driving me wacko!" she mimicked.

"We sound like a couple of babies."

"Okay, baby, let's kiss and make up." She smacked her lips loudly over the wire. "Your turn. I'm waiting."

His father was in the living room. Tod turned his back and smacked his lips into the phone.

"Come on, you call that a kiss?" Hilary said. "I could barely hear it."

"Hilary—"

"Louder!" she insisted, and demonstrated again how it should be done. Then he did it.

# 32

I don't know if this is good or bad, but finally they've got a name for what Amos has. I found out today when I was leaving the hospital. I saw Amy outside the waiting room and I stopped to say hello to her. Her parents were in there talking to Dr. Lasher. She's chief of the medical team that's working on Amos. I've seen her before. Can't miss her in the halls. She must be six feet tall and she always has something purple on under her white jacket. Today it was a purple dress.

Dr. Lasher was saying something about all the tests they'd given Amos. And then she said, "Everything is pointing us in the direction of infectious cardiomyopathy. The enlarged heart, the flulike syndrome, the weakness and shortness of breath—"

"Cardiowhat?" Amos's father said.

"Infectious cardiomyopathy," Dr. Lasher said.

"I never heard of it," Amos's mother said.

"It's a rare viral infection," Dr. Lasher said. "That's the reason we haven't diagnosed it sooner. Nobody else on the team had any previous experience with it. In fifteen years of pediatric practice, I've only seen three other cases."

I wanted to remember everything Dr. Lasher said to tell Tod. She said that Amos's heart was working too hard and not

136

doing the job for him and that was why he was so weak. "The virus attacks the heart, and his heart is not sending the blood he needs to the rest of his body."

Then Amos's mother said, "But now that we know what it is, Doctor, there's a cure, isn't there?"

And Dr. Lasher said, "I hope so."

# 33

"Man, I've had it with this place." Amos pulled off the oxygen mask and tossed it aside. "I'm sick . . . of being sick. I'm going . . . home."

For a moment Tod thought something good—no, something *great* had happened. The doctors had finally found the drugs that would cure Amos. They were going to fix him up. *Good as new,* Tod thought.

"Yeah . . . next week," Amos panted. "Getting out." And he looked at Tod as if he were waiting for Tod's agreement, his encouragement, his belief. As if he were waiting to hear Tod say, *Right, Amos, you're getting out of here. I know it, and you know it, and it's going to happen.* Then looking at Amos's eyes, Tod knew it was only a fantasy. There was something frantic in those eyes, something desperate.

"Hey . . . yeah . . . terrific," Tod said. He had the most awful feeling of having let Amos down.

"I know it's a medical thing," he said to Hilary, "that's why I feel so helpless." He stared out over the playing field. He wanted to do *something* for his friend, and there was nothing he could do.

Amos's "getting out" day had come and gone. He wasn't going anywhere. He wasn't getting any better. Every day when Tod came away from visiting, he felt a little more discouraged, a little more helpless than the day before.

"We just have to keep on visiting him," Hilary said. "And keep up his spirits."

Tod tapped his fingers on the window. "Sure, that's fine, but everyone visits." Was his half hour any better or different than anyone else's? Did it have any special value? He was a body in the room so Amos wasn't alone for that period of time—but if Tod wasn't there, then someone else was. As for his small talk, as he'd seen for himself, Hilary did it far better.

"Where'd this come from?" Tod said, picking up a little wooden bear with movable limbs from the bedside table. He worked the limbs back and forth. "Another member of your zoo."

"That's Puddin'," Amos said.

"Good name. Did Amy give it to you?"

"Hilary. It was . . . her grandmother's."

"It belonged to Nana? She must like you a lot." And right then, Tod understood what he, and only he, could do for Amos.

"You know, old man, Hilary and I had a thing for each other for a few days—"

"Didn't work out?" Amos said.

"Nah!" Tod waved his hand dismissively. "We got bored with each other." He'd barely thought this through, and it was a shock to hear himself saying it. He was giving up Hilary. Giving her up for the duration of Amos's illness.

"You had a fight?" Amos pushed himself up against the pillows.

"Nothing that dramatic. Some people, let's face it, it's chemistry. It's yes or it's no. With us, it was no." Tod watched Amos's face. He could tell he was carrying it off, and for a moment he got very scared. How was he going to explain this to Hilary? And what would they do when Amos got better?

"Didn't you ever wonder why we don't come to see you together?" Tod said. "And why do you think when we do run into each other here, we hardly talk? You noticed, didn't you, Amos?"

Amos nodded.

"I knew you knew something." He had the ball and he was running with it. "I see the way she is with you." He scored with that. Amos's face brightened. "You're more than friends. I've seen her kissing you," Tod went on recklessly. "You can't tell me that doesn't mean something."

"Man," Amos said. "Man . . . you aren't putting me on?"

Tod laid his hand over his heart. A corny gesture. The whole thing was fragile, but Amos bought it. Because he was sick . . . because he wanted it to be true.

"I don't know where the idea came from," Tod said. "It just came into my head that this was the way to make him feel better." He glanced at Hilary, who had been listening without comment. They were in Margo's, passing a piece of pie back and forth. "It's going to help him. It's going to make him happy, right?" She still didn't say anything. "Everyone knows that if you're happy, your immune system works better and your body is stronger and can fight off disease and viruses."

"That's true."

"So what do you think? Are you mad, are you sad, are you glad? What?"

"I ought to be mad. That old thing, just handing me over—"

"Hilary, it's only because he's sick. You know that! I would never have—! And you do like him, that's not a lie."

She put her chin in her hands. "I can see why you did it. It's really a good idea," she mused. "But are you saying we shouldn't see each other *at all* until he's well? In school? How about the phone?"

Faced with it, Tod hesitated. "That seems kind of drastic, doesn't it?"

She pushed the plate across the table to him. "Look, when I'm with Amos or you're with him, I'm going to know and you're going to know we're lying to him about us. And after a while, Amos is going to know, too. And that's going to be bad. If we do this, we have to do it right."

"Meaning?" Tod said.

"We shouldn't see each other until . . ." She hesitated.

"Until Amos is out of the hospital?"

"Until Amos is out of the hospital," she repeated. She stuck out her hand and he shook it to seal their agreement.

# 34

Day by day, moment by moment, Tod saw Hilary and Amos drawn closer together, into a circle of feeling. He was outside that circle, roaming the perimeter, peering in at the two of them from the fringes. And what could he say? How could he protest? How could he complain? He had done this. This was his gift to Amos.

One morning as he dressed, Tod looked out the window, watching a lone silver cloud pass slowly overhead. Was Amos watching the same cloud from his window? Was Hilary? He remembered a childhood fantasy he'd had of riding the clouds, riding to wherever his mother was and bringing her back with him. Now, if he could, he'd scoop up Hilary and they'd ride the cloud together. . . . Then, guiltily, he added Amos. The three of them . . . *We'll ride the cloud forever, Amos, ride it home. . . .*

The hospital smelled of breakfast. The halls were crowded with food gurneys. In Amos's room the curtain was drawn on one side of his bed. Tod started in, then stopped. Hilary was half-sitting, half-lying on the bed, her arms around Amos.

Tod stood there, as if the room were a stage set and Hilary and Amos the actors. *I started this,* he thought, recalling his businesslike handshake with Hilary. *I put them together. I'm the playwright, the creator, the director. The fool.* As he watched, he saw Amos's hand in Hilary's hair. Something thick rose in his throat. He swallowed. A blankness came up in him, rose up like a gray wall that cut out thought, cut out feeling and sensation.

Amos was always in bed now when Tod came to visit, always sucking on the oxygen, always falling asleep in the middle of a sentence.

"They're talking about a heart transplant," Amy told Tod as they left the hospital one day. "He's on the list."

"Does he know?"

"Yes, of course. But somebody with a healthy heart has to die. Then that family has to donate the heart. And then Amos has to be next on the list."

"God," Tod said.

"How long can we wait? When they get a heart, is he going to be strong enough for the operation?"

"Amos wants to live."

"Wanting isn't enough." She started to cry and he put his arm around her.

"Amy . . ."

"No, don't say anything, Tod. . . . It's so hard to accept that what you want and what you get might not be the same thing."

"They're going to find a cure, Amy," he said. She just looked at him. But when they got on the bus she said, "Tod, don't you know the doctors told Mom and Dad there's no cure? The transplant is his only hope."

He looked out the window. The sun bounced off the golden dome of a bank. Another bus passed, puffing out black fumes. Every time he took a breath of air, he thought of Amos. Then he thought of his father's friend, Richie, who had died when he was eighteen. He thought of soldiers everywhere, in all the wars. He thought of all the boys who died young.

He had to go into work that night. It was hard for him to concentrate. Everything he did seemed unimportant, trivial. He kept thinking, Was it true that Amos might die?

He found himself concentrating all his attention on the Eatons, a regular Friday-night couple, both of them hefty and healthy looking. He watched them bowling. He watched them eating and drinking. He watched them taking off their bowling shoes and paying Loretta. In all that time they never spoke to each other, they never touched.

He wanted them to touch. It seemed unbearable that they didn't touch. He couldn't shake the thought that if they didn't touch, everything was lost. And he thought of Hilary and of himself. And then he thought of Amos. And he was frightened.

"Where's Hilary?" Amos said. "I thought . . . she was coming to see me today."

"Was she?" Tod went to the door and looked down the hall. Hilary was walking quickly toward him, pushing her hair off her face. "She's coming now, Amos," he said. He went to the bed. "I better get going. Okay, buddy?"

Hilary came in and she and Tod glanced at each other. She was wearing Amos's double-heart locket.

Amos raised a hand in farewell to Tod. Or was it dismissal? It was a royal gesture, and the thought flashed through Tod's mind that Amos's illness had put a crown on him. Nobody could refuse him anything anymore.

In the hall he heard the murmur of Hilary's voice and then Amos's. Then silence. He didn't go back. He didn't look in. He didn't have to. He didn't want to. He didn't need to. He knew what he would see, he imagined everything, and it made him crazy.

# 35

When Tod got to the hospital Sunday morning, Amos's bed was empty and stripped of linen. His things were gone. The table next to the bed was wiped clean. Nothing, not a sign of him. No food, no flowers, no cards. Bozo, the IV, was gone. King Kong, the oxygen tank, was gone. Even Puddin', Hilary's little bear, was gone.

Tod ran out to the nurses' station. "Where is he?"

"Who?" a nurse said. He didn't recognize her.

"Amos." He could hardly speak. "Vaccaro."

"Vaccaro?" she said.

What was the matter with her? Amos had been here for weeks. Tod stared at a sign on the wall: I'M NOT HAVING A NERVOUS BEARDOWN. THIS IS THE WAY I ALWAYS LOOK. *Beardown?* He looked again and the letters blurred. "Amos Vaccaro," he repeated. "Where is he? His bed—"

She flipped through a chart. "Vaccaro, Amos. Moved to intensive care. Fifth floor."

Tod stood at the door of the intensive care room. There were five beds in the room, and in each bed he saw a humped figure, a beaked nose, a huddle of bones

146

under white sheets. Amos looked lost in his bed, small, shrunken, and old. Yes, he looked old. He'd aged. He could have been forty years old, or a hundred.

Tod stepped back. He didn't want to go in. There was a foul smell in the air, a choking thick smell. He couldn't breathe. He made himself go to the bed. "Hi," he said to Amos. "You sleeping?"

Amos rolled his head *no* against the pillow.

Tod leaned over and took Amos's hand. There was a tube in his nose, another taped to the back of his hand. He was surrounded by monitors and machines. A doctor was being paged. The room was noisy. Machines whirred, beeped, chugged. There was no quiet here, no peace. Nurses came and went, and overhead there was the constant chatter of the intercom. "Doctor Greenwald . . . Doctor James Greenwald, you are wanted in pediatrics. Doctor Lissom, Doctor Phyllis Lissom, please go to X-ray."

Amos tried to push himself up in the bed, and the covers fell away. More wires were taped to his chest. "How are you, my man?" he whispered.

"Okay. I see they got you all wired up in here."

"Wired . . . and retired . . ." Amos's eyelids trembled. "My best friend," he whispered. "I love you, man."

Tod's eyes filled. "Hey, Amos . . . let me get you some water." At the sink in the corner he filled the water pitcher.

"Tod . . . Tod . . . ," Amos called in his whispery voice.

"I'm here. I'm right here, Amos." He put down the water pitcher.

"Want to tell you something. I'm getting out . . . soon."

"You bet you're getting out," Tod said. His voice was

loud, even in that noisy room. "And the first thing we do is make a huge party for you."

"Party . . . sure . . ." A shadow of Amos's old eager smile crossed his face. Words seemed to tremble on his lips. Then his eyes closed.

Tod sat next to him, watching him sleep, watching his eyes waver under his lids. Remembering Amos as he had been only a few weeks ago. Thinking how Amos would once have responded.

*A party, man? Hey, great! You're going to come, you and Hilary, and all my friends. Remember that cute girl, Katie? And how about Jen, the one you wanted me to fall for? Invite everybody, we're going to celebrate! Man, are the nurses going to be happy to see me go. They've tried every which way they know to get rid of me. Maybe we should invite them, too!*

Amos moved in his sleep. Tod watched him. *Wake up, Amos. I'm talking to you, Amos . . . listen . . . please listen . . .*

*I hear you, man. Do you think I'm sick? Ha! Fooled you, didn't I? Great act, isn't it? Man, would I crap out on you? You know I wouldn't. Am I leaving this place? You know I am.*

Tod leaned over him. He wanted Amos to sit up, if only for a moment. He wanted to see him the way he'd always been. He wanted him to smile that smile of his. He wanted to tear off those damn wires and see Amos walk out of there.

# 36

In the woods, Tod saw blue sky through the bare branches. The air was filled with the smell of leaves. Hilary was ahead of him on the narrow path. She stumbled, and Tod tried to steady her, but she plunged on. He thought she was crying.

"Hilary—"

"No!"

A fallen tree blocked the path. She kicked the tree. "Damn!" She sat down on the ground. Amos's locket swung against her sweater.

Tod sat down next to her. "I shouldn't have called you."

"Why? That's stupid! You had to call me. And it's stupid of me to be so weepy. Be real, Hilary!" She pounded her fists on her thighs. "Be real! What good does crying do Amos? Does it get him out of intensive care? Does it make him any better?"

A flurry of leaves filled the air.

She wiped her eyes and sighed. "If we stayed here long enough, do you think the leaves would cover us?"

"It would have to be an awfully long time."

"We could just sit here. Sit here without moving. Like this." She froze into place, her hands in midair. "'As good as dead."

He leaned his forehead against hers. "Come on," he said, "come on, come on . . ."

"Oh, God, do you realize we're doing it, Tod? Breaking our promise to ourselves? We're *together*! How can we ever face him?"

"It's okay," he said. "Just this once. We had to talk. I had to see you."

"I don't want to talk anymore. I don't want to talk about anything. I don't want to think. I don't want to be unhappy. Please! I don't want to be unhappy!"

He felt her lips against his. He put his arms around her neck. They looked at each other. "Oh, you have such beautiful brown eyes," she said. She was half-weeping and half-laughing.

# 37

"Tod." It was Amy on the phone. "You'd better come to the hospital if you want to see Amos."

"Amy—"

"Just come," she said. "I'm calling everybody."

When Tod walked into the hospital room, Hilary was already there. "Hello," he whispered to her. They stood by the bed, on opposite sides. "Amos," Tod said, bending toward him, "I'm here, old man."

Amos's eyes opened. He seemed to have trouble waking up. His face was puffy and swollen. His eyelids were almost black. He looked from Hilary to Tod. Did he recognize them? He said something, and Tod bent over him. "What? I'm here, Amos."

"He wants you to hold his hand," Hilary said.

Tod took Amos's hand.

"I'm here," he said.

Amos's lids fluttered. He held his other hand out to Hilary, then, slowly, his arms trembling with the effort, he brought Tod's and Hilary's hands together.

His eyes closed, but he held on to their hands.

Tod and Hilary stayed there, bent awkwardly over him, until the nurse came in and sent them away.

\*     \*     \*

Early the next morning Tod called Amy. The phone was busy for a long time. When he finally got through, he said, "Amy, it's Tod. How is he?"

There was silence. Then she said, "Tod. Tod. Tod . . ."

Her older brother Nick got on the phone. "Our brother, our Amos . . . he died from heart failure last night."

Tod said something. It seemed important to keep his voice steady, to say something. But later he couldn't remember what he had said.

He called Hilary. "I know," she said. "I heard." And she hung up.

The day of the funeral Hilary was absent from school. Tod left around noon, waited outside a few moments for the bus, then impatient, afraid he would be late, he started walking. He walked hard, unzipping his jacket, then taking it off. He was sweating by the time he got to the cemetery.

A line of cars and school buses were parked along the edge of the road. He walked between the gravestones toward the crowd. A big group of kids from Bishop Hayes were there in their school uniforms. He saw Katie from the drama club and the two football players who'd come to the hospital. Hilary was there, too, standing with the Vaccaros. He raised his hand in a muted greeting, but her eyes slid away.

At the end of the ceremony a lot of the kids from Amos's school were crying. Some were on their knees, praying. Tod watched Hilary throw something bright into the open grave. *The locket,* he thought.

As people started to leave, he went up to Amos's

parents. Hilary and Amy were in the limousine already. "Mrs. Vaccaro," Tod said. "I'm so—"

She lifted her veil to kiss him. "My boy always loved you," she said.

After everyone had left, he watched the workmen fill in the grave with the backhoe, then throw a green carpet over the bare earth and replace the wreaths and flowers. Then they put their shovels in the back of a truck and drove away.

Tod went to the edge of the grave. A car drove slowly past. He stood warming his hands in his pockets.

"You're dead, Amos." He kicked away the corner of the plastic carpet. "You're dead in the ground. I'm never going to see you again. You're gone." And then he felt an enormous swelling of anger and betrayal. Was everyone he loved always going to leave him? "Goddamn it!" He kicked furiously at the dirt.

He had thought he knew a lot about dying. Hadn't he almost died? And his mother had died. And he'd heard his father talk about Richie more times than he could count. He'd thought the painful part was while it was happening. Afterward, what was there to say? The dead were dead. They were gone and they didn't come back. That was it. It was a one-way trip. No return ticket. And the people left behind learned to live with it. That was what he had thought.

Dying . . . what was it really? Was Amos really in that hole? His body, yes, but where was Amos? Maybe he had gotten into a car, the official black death car, and he had driven off. A nice little story. And why not? Better to think of Amos buzzing along a highway than lying in that stinking coffin. And maybe along the way he'd even meet Tod's mother in her black car.

*Cute, Tod. What are they going to do, meet at a rest stop? Talk over a cup of coffee? Sure.* And Amos would mention his friend Tod. And his mother would say she had a son by that name. Great. They'd have something in common. Amos would like that story, he thought.

He stood there for a while looking down at the plastic carpet. The wind came up and gusted, and he zipped up his jacket. The sky had turned a bright, cold blue. "Good-bye, Amos," he said at last. "Good-bye, brother. Good-bye, my friend."

# 38

Hilary and Tod went out together a few times after Amos died. It didn't work. They weren't close. They were awkward together. It wasn't the way it had been in the beginning, easy and shining between them. Tod kept wanting to talk about Amos and suppressing it, because Hilary tightened up when his name was mentioned. "I don't have to talk about him," she said. "I have my memories."

Tod had his memories, too. He remembered that moment at the falls when long ago he knew he was going to hit the rocks. Amos had saved him. Now Amos was dead—and Tod hadn't been able to save him.

Every time he was with Hilary, Amos was there, too. Every time Tod touched Hilary, he felt Amos behind him, Amos's shadow, whatever it was, hovering there. And whether he was with Hilary or alone, Tod talked constantly to Amos, explaining about Hilary and him, how things had happened, and especially how he had never wanted to hurt Amos. Never. Never, never, never.

One day, almost dutifully, he said, "We shouldn't feel guilty because Amos is dead and we're alive, Hilary."

155

"Yes, I know."

"We shouldn't feel guilty because we were in the woods that day."

"I know—" She fell silent.

"We shouldn't feel guilty because of the way we met, either."

"I know! I know you're right, but it's just words, isn't it?"

It was true. With Amos dead it was as if what had been alive between them, all that feeling, that light, that shining thing, was also dead.

He and Hilary stopped going out. In school they passed each other in the halls with quick waves and evasive smiles.

One night he called her house. "I'll see if she's home," Paula said. "Hold on." He heard Paula calling, and he imagined her going up the stairs, through the hall, into the attic, into Hilary's room. And in his mind, the room was empty.

He wasn't at all surprised when Paula returned to say, "Tod? Hilary's gone out. I'll tell her you called."

He wasn't at all surprised when Hilary didn't call back.

Whenever he saw her in school, she was always in a hurry, always standing on one foot. "I've only got a second," she'd say, and she'd have one hand on his arm, but not to bring him close—holding him off, talking fast, giving him bits of news. Flash! Paula was going to do her last two years at St. Lawrence University. Flash! Carl wanted Hilary to work more hours at the garage! Flash! Her family was putting pressure on her again about college.

"I'm on my way to guidance right now to search through college catalogs. My ambition is to be the first grease monkey with a Ph.D." She was cheerful, she was friendly, but she was never available.

Only once she suddenly said, as if in the middle of an argument, "We couldn't go on as if nothing had happened! You can see that!" And then she walked away.

After that, when he saw her, when he could get her to stop even for those few seconds, he would search her eyes, but there was never anything there about Tod and Hilary.

"I've been thinking," his father said. "Remember when we talked about smoking?" Tod nodded. They were in the car, on the way home from eating out. "Did I hear you say you wanted me to stop?"

"Yes." Tod looked out the window at the black trees moving by. He thought of Amos. Again and again he thought of Amos. Again and again the shiver of guilt: that Amos was dead and he was alive. *Amos . . . Why you? Why not me? I could have died. Why not? The virus got you, but it could have been me. It was chance. An accident. Bad luck. Amos. . . .*

"Would it mean something to you if I did stop smoking?" his father was saying.

Tod looked at his father. "What? Oh, sure . . . Yes."

His father took the pack he'd just opened and threw it out the window.

"You've got plenty more at home," Tod said. Unexpectedly his eyes smarted. He hadn't cried at the funeral, and he hadn't cried since then. Now he started. "I don't know what's the matter with me," he said, choking.

His father pulled over to the side of the road. "Easy, old man. . . . Is it Amos?" Tod nodded, and his father put his arm around him, held him hard. Tod grabbed him, and then he really started bawling.

# 39

There were times that winter when Tod felt an ache up and down his left side, pins and needles, as if his body had fallen asleep on that side. Sometimes he wondered if something bad was happening to him. Sometimes he felt it like a numbness, as if something were missing, and then he understood. He knew what was missing. Amos. Hilary.

Once when the phone rang, Tod picked it up and said, "Amos?" And then he remembered.

He walked past Carl's Automotive and looked inside. Hilary was in back. The radio was on. "I've been up," a man sang, "and down . . . and all around . . . can't find you nowhere, darlin' . . ."
Tod didn't go in. He stood there for a moment only, then went on.

On his wall he tacked up the picture of the three of them that they'd taken at the State Fair. There they were—Hilary, Amos, Tod—smiling and leaning into each other.

How long ago had that been? Only three months? There was Hilary with her level, unambiguous look, the gaze that said, What you see is what you get. And Amos, his chin in Tod's shoulder, grinning that ready smile full of feeling. And himself—smiling, too, but guardedly, a smile like his father's.

New Year's Day, Tod walked through frozen fields to the falls. A lot of rain had fallen, and the water spilled down in a muddy flow. He'd never been here in the winter before. The water tossed rocks and boulders around like marbles. Stones tumbled and knocked against each other. And under the uproar, under the commotion, he seemed to hear Amos's voice greeting him.

Tod and Jen went downtown one day to see the mural. Tod wanted to see if Amos was still there in the "window," still holding the trumpet.

Jen said, "I'm disappointed. It doesn't look like Amos at all."

Tod moved closer to the mural, saw the bricks and lost the effect of the picture, then moved away again— and there was Amos. Not Amos the way he'd been those last days, lost in the bed, but Amos with his cheeks puffed out and shining, Amos with the trumpet raised cockily to his lips.

Once he thought he saw Amos through the window of a store, a dim figure looking out.

Another time he suddenly "saw" Amos in the backseat of a car. He looked at Tod as the car passed, and Tod raised his hand in greeting and farewell.

# 40

Tod graduated that spring. For a few months he worked with Loretta in her new business, cleaning offices. He was the window-washing specialist. He liked the monotony of the work: it gave him a chance to think, or not think. Should he go to college? Should he wait? Should he forget it? The thought of sitting in classrooms for another four years of his life didn't appeal to him. Or maybe it was that the life with his father had gotten into his blood. He wanted to travel. Only he didn't want to go across town, but across the country or across an ocean.

Amos's death had brought things up in his mind. He thought a lot about love, that word that people used that meant so many different things. When you heard the word and you weren't going through it, you thought it meant happiness. And you thought happiness meant love. As if they were interchangeable.

He thought about Hilary and Amos, and how the three of them had come together and then been torn apart. Everything was complex. Things happened that you couldn't have foreseen. Sometimes you did things wrong and felt lousy. Sometimes you did things right

160

and thought you had all the loose ends tied up . . . and then everything unraveled.

One evening he sat down and wrote a letter to his grandmother in England. She lived in a little town called Royston between London and Cambridge. "They used to be farmers," his father said. "I remember your mother saying so. I think they still do something with animals. That's up your alley."

"Dear Mrs. Todman," Tod began. He crossed that out and started again. "Dear Grandmother, I hope you are well. You and my grandfather both. I know I've never written you before, and I hope it's okay that I'm writing now. Do you still remember me? I'm Tod Ellerbee, your grandson. I'm nearly eighteen years old, and I've recently graduated from high school. Right now I have money saved, and I've been thinking seriously about coming to England and meeting my mother's family.

"Maybe you will have things to tell me about my mother. My other family—besides my father, I mean—is spread all over the United States. My father's father lives in Houston, Texas, and I have an aunt in California. Sometime I want to visit them, too, but right now I think I would rather go to England. Who knows when I can do it again? I will look forward to your reply." And he signed it, "Your grandson, Tod Ellerbee."

He told himself not to expect anything. It had just been something to do. If nothing came of it, he'd start college. But then a letter came from England.

Dear Tod,

It is a pleasure to me to write this letter. It was so unexpected hearing from you. What a lovely surprise! Of course we didn't forget you. We think about you often, my dear. Many times, many many times, I have wondered where you are and what you're doing. What kind of young man you are. My Rosalie's son. Are you coming here, really, to see us? How wonderful. Your grandfather is not in good health. He will be so pleased to see you. Write me soon again,

With loving devotion,
your grandmother, Mary Todman

# 41

Tod said good-bye to Hilary at her house. She came out on the porch and they stood there talking for a few minutes. "Write me," she said. "I think it's wonderful that you're doing this."

He felt the warmth of her hands on his shoulders. Then their arms went around each other. They hugged for a long time.

His father and Loretta drove Tod to the airport. He was flying to New York, where he'd make his connection for British Airways. Outside the airport Loretta took his picture. "I had to practically break my son's arm to get the camera away from him," she said. "Hold still, Tod. Smile! Okay, Bob, let's get one with you two together. Come on, guys, arms around each other."

She and his father went as far as security with Tod, and then there was the whole awkward business of saying good-bye again. "Don't forget to come back," Loretta said.

"But give me plenty of warning," his father joked.

"Don't forget to write," Loretta said.

"You got that notebook?" His father's travel gift had

been a notebook. He wanted Tod to keep a record of his trip.

"I want a postcard from England, at least," Loretta said.

"Right, right." Tod kept looking around, hoping that Hilary would appear. He imagined it like a scene from a movie. Or was it one of those beer commercials? Hilary, running toward him, her hair floating, feet barely touching the ground. Tod! Tod! I couldn't let you go without telling you I love you!

His father shook his hand for about the tenth time. And for about the tenth time Loretta said, "Bob! Hug him."

Tod dropped his knapsack on the security ramp. On the other side, just before he turned out of sight, he looked back. Loretta waved. His father had already turned away. Walking down the long carpeted tunnel leading to the gate, Tod realized that he and his father had never been separated before.

In New York he had a four-hour layover at Kennedy Airport. He went by one bank of phones after another and thought about calling Hilary. He went into a cafeteria and ate and then walked again and passed the phones another dozen times. In a gift shop he bought postcards and a little ceramic sculpture—a boy and a girl in old-fashioned costumes sitting on a log. Maybe he'd send it to Hilary.

After a while he sat down and tried to write something about leaving everyone and everything he knew, venturing into the unknown. The unknown? That was pushing it a little. Going to his grandparents in Royston, England, wasn't exactly climbing Mt. Everest or heading into the Antarctic.

On the plane he had a window seat. He watched the

land fall away, saw the land end, and then they were over the ocean. He saw ships below, but as the plane climbed, they got smaller and smaller, until they looked like tiny silver arrows. He leaned back.

He fell asleep and dreamed that he saw Hilary and Amos. He started toward them. He had to tell them something important. He tried to run, but he could only move slowly. Then he noticed that he was in the water, and he saw two little stocky figures on the shore, holding out their hands to him. It was his grandparents. He swam toward them.

When he woke up, he started on his postcards. Jen, first. "Hi, cutie . . . writing this above the clouds. Don't forget me when I'm far away. And listen, I forgot to say this, but it's important. I really love you."

To his father he wrote, "Dad, I'm watching you. I've got my informants. You smoke and I'll know it. No smoking!"

Then to Loretta: "I hope you find another super window-washer!"

He wrote cards to Mrs. Vaccaro, Mrs. Pace, Amy, even Scott. ("Hi, Scott, so far everything's going great.")

He kept Hilary for last. What would he say to her? What should he say to her? Everything, he thought. But then he only wrote, "Someday, Hilary . . . someday . . ." He wanted to write more, but he felt that everything was in that one word. *Someday. . . .*

## ABOUT THE AUTHORS

Award-winning novelists NORMA FOX MAZER and HARRY MAZER team up for the second time in their careers with *Heartbeat*. Their first collaboration, *The Solid Gold Kid*, is available in a Starfire paperback edition. Norma has written seventeen books and is the author of *After the Rain*, a Newbery Honor book for 1988. Harry, who has written thirteen books, is the author of *The Girl of His Dreams*, which was named a Best Book by the American Library Association. They have four grown children and live near Syracuse, New York.